End Game

PLAYING FOR KEEPS
BOOK THREE

SAMANTHA BARRETT

For my dirty girls,
For all my girls that like to act like a queen in the street but fuck like
a freak in the sheets.
Get a man that knows how to fuck you so hard you walk with a
limp, if he doesn't make you squirt then onto the next, boo.

PROLOGUE

Beckett

You can take the rat out of the sewer but you can't take the sewer out of the rat.

Most people hate rats. They call them rodents, a menace but what they don't realize about us rats, is that we are fucking resilient. You lay traps to catch us, bait us with the food we crave, tempt us to come out of the shadows, you think we're just dumb rodents. I'm here to fucking tell you that we are anything but dumb. We are smart, cunning, and fearsome because we know what it's like to have nothing, so when we fight for what we want, we don't give up.

I may be the rat but Valance Karver is the cat. She's the one who tried to lure me out of the shadows. She thought she was the predator and I was the prey, she was so fucking wrong, I showed her what happens when a rat is backed into a corner with nowhere to go. We will fight to the death, and claw our way out of any situation.

I showed her what happens when you back *me* into a corner that night I killed her father. What I didn't expect when I left her behind that night was for her to show up years later with my four-year-old son, threatening to take him from me. She thinks she knows me. Nah, she knew the old me who had nothing—no home, no parents, and nothing else to care for except her.

She's about to meet the new Beckett Dawson. The one who is cutthroat and willing to play dirty to get what he wants. I'll ruin everything she holds near and dear to her black heart for keeping my son from me.

CHAPTER ONE

Beckett

Four years ago

I jump through her open bedroom window and immediately the sound of shouting hits my ears. I fucking hate her piece of shit father. Her mother is just as bad, she allows this shit to happen to her own daughter. I grind my teeth and clench my fists at my sides, trying with all my might to keep my composure and not go out there and beat the fat piece of shit myself.

"You best get that shit fixed up fast, little girl, or else." I close my eyes, trying to block out the sound of his voice, I've told her time and time again to run away with me. I can't keep staying in this town, I'm bound to get caught soon and I ain't going into the fucking system. I'd rather take my chances on the streets. I had to drop out of school this week because social services called them about me. Mrs. Patterson —my homeroom teacher—gave me a heads up, she even gave me fifty bucks to get me some food. I've kept that money close to me for four days, it's going to pay for mine and Valance's bus ticket outta this fucking place.

"Yes, sir. I'll fix it up now." The tremble in her voice cuts me deep, she is fucking petrified of her father. He's nothing but a fucking useless piece of shit. He lost his job a few years ago when the old mill on Johnson Road shut down. He's been on a pension ever since and drinks away their money. If he isn't drinking it, then he sure as fuck is chewing it. The cunt makes Val scrub out the spit stains on the carpet from his tobacco. He is a poor ass excuse for a father and a man. He constantly lays hands on Valance and her mother does nothing. She just sits there and watches as her daughter gets beaten. She'd rather say nothing and allow this to continue than risk his anger turning on her and receiving the same punishment.

"You fucking idiot! I said over there," he shouts. I hear something shatter then a scream tears from Val. I try to block it out, but every time I bring up her father and what he does, she gets pissed off. She hates him but won't allow me to share in that hate.

"I'm sorry," she cries out, and the sound of glass shattering has me taking a step toward the door. I war within myself on whether I should stay out of it as she has always told me to or do the right thing and give him a taste of his own medicine.

"No, but you will be." The icy tone of his voice fills me with dread. I hear her begin to sob and my chest aches.

"Mama, please," Val begs. Her father's laughter is dark and dreary, sending a cold tingle down my spine.

"She won't help you. She learned the hard way and now so will you." A *crack* sounds out followed by a pained scream from Val.

Stay out of it, she has warned you to never step in!

I try to repeat that over and over in my head but when I register what is making that *cracking* sound, my whole-body thrums with the need to inflict pain. I grip her door handle still trying to talk myself out of it, then she screams again, but this time she calls for help and I'm powerless to stop myself from tearing her bedroom door open. I storm down the tiny hallway that opens into the filthy living room. The sight that greets me is gruesome. Valance is on the floor, hands over her face and tucked into a fetal position as her father stands over her trembling body striking her with his belt. I dart my gaze to the couch in the corner where her mother sits, puffing on a cigarette while staring at the TV.

"Fucking cunt, you'll learn to do as you're told you good for nothing bitch!" That's it, his words hurl me into action. I charge forward tackling him from the side, a scream tears from her poor ass excuse of a mother. Ronald grunts as he hits the floor, fueled by my anger and blinded by the need to teach him a lesson of my own, I flip him onto his back and straddle his legs. His eyes widen in shock at the sight of me. Before a single word can be uttered from his mouth, I clock his jaw with a right hook, followed up by a left.

I keep this up until my arms feel like lead, his face is busted and bloody but anger still courses through my veins. I look to my left to find his discarded belt. I push off him and grip the belt before wrapping it around my hand, leaving the buckle end dangling. I hear muffled sobs from behind me but don't dare look. Valance can be pissed all she likes but I'm doing this for her, if she chooses not to come with me at least I'll know she is safe.

I rear my arm back, ready to strike him but falter at the sound of Valance's plea. "Beckett, don't." I peer over my shoulder, the sight of her bloody face, the split skin on her arms and the welts on her legs has a rage like I have never felt before tearing through me. I swing my gaze back to the unconscious piece of shit on the floor, a groan tumbles from his busted lips and that simple sound snaps me back to the task at hand. This time when I ready to strike, I ignore her pleas and I whip him as hard as I can with the belt buckle. Everything becomes white noise, the sounds of her pleas, the cries of her mother fade to nothing, I don't even see clearly anymore. It's like I've retreated so far inside myself that I am no longer in control and my body is acting upon its desires. I feel no pain, no anger just… nothingness and it's fucking euphoric.

Pain explodes in the back of my head, ripping me from my blissed-out state, I stumble forward and catch myself on the edge of the old worn-out recliner Val's father normally sits in. I reach up and press my hand against the back of my head hissing as pain explodes. I pull my hand away and frown when blood coats my fingers. I slowly turn around to see Valance standing there with tears rolling down her cheeks, glass littering the place I was just standing—she hit me over the head with a vase!

"What the fuck have you done?" Val screams so loud I almost shrink back. Her mother leaps off her perch on the couch and crawls toward her husband's unconscious body sobbing. Lynette grips his shoulders and begins to shake him. I cringe at the ungodly sight of him. His face looks like it has been shredded, his arms are coated in blood, the white singlet he wears now torn and stained red.

"Ron!" Lynette cries as she continues to shake him. "Wake up, you have to wake up!" Valance darts her piercing sky blue eyes at me, they're filled with pain and fear. She drops to her knees beside her mother and reaches out to place two fingers against his neck, feeling for a pulse. I want to roll my eyes, the asshole is just out cold from getting a taste of his own medicine.

"He's dead." Two words, that's all it took to shift my whole world upside down and set me on a path I never saw coming.

CHAPTER TWO

Beckett

Now

The sight of the cabin we purchased nearly three years ago has a sense of belonging flowing through me. This is the only place I can truly call mine–ours—but same thing. I've never had a place to call my own, with this cabin I know I will never have to sleep under another bridge or feel the bite of the cold snow against my skin as I struggle to find warmth.

Darius rides his Ducati in front of Corvin's car with me taking up the rear in my car. I'm so fucking ready to hang out over the Christmas break and just chill with my brothers and the girls. Leah, Cody, Katie, and one of Leah's other friends will be coming up tomorrow after they finish their final assignments. Parking my car in front of the garage, I step out and breathe in the fresh scent of pine. The wind has a bite to it as I blow out a breath and smirk at the cloud of smoke that lingers in front of my face.

"It's fucking freezing!" Saint bites out as he rubs his hands together, and heads to the trunk of Corv's car to grab the bags. I meet Nathan at the back of mine and help him and Crue grab the bags out. We packed most of the food in my car and stuffed the bags in Corv's. I love being here at the cabin, but when it's winter it always pays to go overboard with the food shopping in case we get snowed in, which happens more often than not. Nathan nudges his way past me as I shake my head. Leah seems to think he has slotted in with us easily but it's not that simple. Yeah, he seems cool and we all get along with him for Leah's sake, but trust and loyalty are earned and he has a long was to go. The dude has the best of both worlds. He can hang with the girls and the guys. I know Darius still eyes him whenever he's near Leah, which is fucking stupid. Nathan has admitted more than a dozen times he would rather fuck Darius or Saint, the man prefers sausage to bun. He isn't unashamed of his sexuality and embraces who is without reservation. I envy him. His green eyes shine with life, and his multi-colored brown and blond hair is always a mess but he makes it work. He's a big guy and should be on the team. When we offered him a tryout spot, he looked Darius right in the eyes and said *'the only balls I want to catch from you are in your pants'*, we haven't tried again.

I follow after the others and the moment I step inside, a shiver runs down my spine. I didn't realize how cold I was until I stepped inside the cabin. Corvin heads straight for the fireplace in the sunken living room. I help cart the groceries into the kitchen where Crue and Saint are already unloading the bags they brought in. We make quick work of stacking the butler's pantry, fridge and cupboards. I leave the five of them to do whatever the hell they want while I grab my bags and head up to my room, which is next to Darius's. I shoulder my door open and stand at the entrance for a minute as I take in the space that is mine. It took me over a year to add any personal touches to the room.

"Yo, you want in on pizza, *Becky*?" I grit my teeth and take a calming breath before I drop my bags in the doorway and move to the banister. Leaning over, I see Darius smirking up at me.

"You want to hear your girl screaming *Becky* when she comes?" The smirk drops off his face, I hear the other's laughter from the living room causing my lips to lift at the corner.

"You're a fucking prick!" Darius growls, his words lack the burn and his coffee-colored eyes hold no anger. He is the epitome of a bad boy. Darius has the look nailed—dark eyes, black hair, and always sporting a glower. The girls flock to him because of the dark vibes he gives off. Except they are pushing shit uphill, Darius has only had eyes for one girl, the only one he has ever let in and loved completely. His love for Leah nearly destroyed our chosen family. The moment Corvin took a step back and realized his best friend wasn't just *fucking* his little sister, but was madly in love with Leah and would do whatever it took to keep her, he let go of his anger and alas, here we are.

"We all know you have a prick and I got a bigger dick, just ask *Goldie*." I throw the nickname he uses for Leah at him and smile wide. He grits his teeth and within a second he is racing up the stairs. I shift and brace for impact as he charges at me. The moment he tackles me to the ground we both burst out laughing. He rests back straddling my legs, and punches me in the gut, pulling a groan from me.

"One fucking time I let you play with us and you constantly use it against me." He tries to keep his tone light but the regretful look in his eyes betrays him. He regrets ever letting me fuck her. I knew he wasn't in the right frame of mind that night, I also knew he was trying to prove to himself that she didn't mean shit to him. Except, the moment I slid inside her I saw the look in his eyes.

"I'm sorry." He frowns down at me. "I knew you would regret that night, in my own way I was trying to push you so you would see that she is meant for you. I never should have let shit get that far but…"

"She pulled you out of the shadows as well," he whispers.

I nod, unable to lie to him. He sighs and drops to his ass leaning back against the banister and I slide into a sitting position and lean against the wall behind me. I bend my knee and rest my arm atop it.

"I'll never mention it again," I say, meaning it.

He shakes his head and lulls it to the side facing me. "I'm not mad about it, I just…" He cuts himself off sliding a hand down his face. He doesn't need to put it into words, I get it.

"Hate the thought of me knowing what she likes and looks like without clothes, I get it." He eyes me warily, we've never spoken like this before and it's fucking weird but also… freeing in a sense. "That night brought us closer–"

"Do you still have feelings for her?" He cuts in. I see it in his eyes, this question has been burning in the back of his mind for months. When shit hit the fan with him and Leah, I put her ass on a plane and sent her to Alaska to one of our resorts. I spoke to her daily while she ignored all his and Corvin's attempts to contact her. I was the one she leaned on when they abandoned her. I know that kills him but he needs to let it go or it will cause nothing but problems between her and him.

"I love her." His eyes harden as his body turns ridged. "Not in the way you do but in the way a brother would love a sister. She is… important to me." His brows pinch in the center of his face making his brows raise like *Wolverines*. "Darius, you have nothing to worry about. Leah only sees you, I knew from the second she came to CHU and saw the two of you together that there is a chemistry so strong, I don't know how Corv missed it." Leah means a lot to me because, like someone from my past, she was able to break down my walls and pull me out of the shadows.

"Really?" I smile and nod.

"Dude, the moment she walks into a room your eyes find her without a thought. Even in the dark, she is able to sense you and find you no matter where you hide. The both of you are linked, connected in a way I've never seen before."

Liar. I quiet that fucking annoying voice in the back of my mind.

We're all in the hot tub with a beer in each of our hands. Darius surprised us all tonight by having more than two, he's currently on his fourth. The six of us have been laughing and talking shit most of the evening when the sound of Ella Mai's "Whatchamacallit" breaks through the night. We smirk, while Corv rolls his eyes as D leaps over the side of the tub and races for his phone on the table.

"Hey, Goldie," he says as he answers the call. Corvin pretends to gag and earns a slap up the back of the head from Nathan. Darius's conversation is drowned out when Corvin and Nathan begin to argue. I shake my head and catch a glimpse of Crue's hand disappearing inside Saint's. I keep my gaze on the two arguing in front of me ,not wanting to let on that I know what the other two are doing. Pride swells inside me, about time Crue came clean and told Saint how he feels. Anyone with eyes could see that Crue has been in love with Saint for years. I guess it just took the latter longer to catch on. The thing that stuns me most is, how the hell does Katie fit into their duo?

"The fuck!" Darius's angry shout has us all turning toward him. Corvin pushes toward the edge with worry lines marring his face.

"What the fuck happened?" Corv snaps. Darius stops his pacing and snaps his gaze to his friend, the moment his eyes collide with Corvin's, I laugh. I can feel the other's eyes on me and shake my head. Everyone begins to click on to what I'm laughing at, well everyone except Corv. "The fuck is so funny, asshole?" he grits out.

"Don't make him say it, my dude!" Saint hedges but Corvin ignores him.

"Spit it the fuck out!" The other three guys laugh again at Corvin's poorly chosen words. I decide *fuck it*, if he wants to know so bad, I'll tell him.

"Bet ya a hundred bucks Darius is pissed because Leah is *coming* without him." He frowns for a second and then his eyes widen as a horrified look flashes across his face. He turns to Darius, only to find him whisper shouting in the opposite corner of us.

"Darius!" D snaps his gaze toward a seething Corvin, he grins but it falls off his face the moment Corvin stands in the hot tub.

"Dammit, baby, I gotta go, Your brother is *big* mad." He laughs and quickly ends the call as Corv tries to leap out of the tub. Saint and Crue hold him back.

"I fucking told you never to do that shit in front of me." I tune out their bickering, close my eyes and lean my head back, staring up at the night sky. The stars shine so brightly out here and as much as I hate to admit it, they always remind me of *her*. I don't often think of her anymore, I suppressed all the memories and feelings I felt toward her a long ass time ago. I swore after that night, I would never allow myself to ever love another woman. I may love Leah, but not in the way I loved her. She was my gravity, my reason to remain grounded and fight for a better life. My heart beat only for her until she ripped it out and destroyed me. I didn't go off the rails and change myself as Darius did, I just... closed myself off and never allowed myself to feel anything for anyone except my family.

It's been nearly five years since I have seen her and yet, I can still remember every detail about her perfect face. Her striking blue eyes make you believe she is staring right into your soul, her rich auburn hair that shines red in the sunlight, her explosive personality and that sinfully sexy body. Sometimes I let my mind wander to what she may look like now, I know with age her beauty would have only grown. I snap my eyes open and mentally berate myself for allowing my mind to wander down that dead-end track. She's dead to me and never coming back! If I ever saw her again, I'd make her wish it was her that died that night instead of her piece of shit father.

CHAPTER THREE

"Come on, munchkin, you need to get ready so Momma can get to school." Dawson stares up at me with eyes that resemble my own, he may have my eyes but everything else is *him*. The color of his hair, the smile, the way he struts around like he is the king of this place. I love how strong-willed, determined, and loving he is. Dawson has the biggest heart. I may struggle being a single mom and run on next to no sleep, but I wouldn't change my life. My son is the driving force behind why I push myself so hard to achieve better, want more and never settle. I refuse to allow Dawson to grow up as I did. He will know he is loved and wanted more than anything in this world, even if his father isn't in the picture.

"I no want go school, Momma." Sighing, I drop down in front of the threadbare sofa that he sits on and grip his tiny hands in mine. I hate that I have to leave him and go to school or work but, unfortunately, I don't have another choice. Being a single mom was not something I thought I would ever have to deal with, kids were never on the cards for me. I just never had the urge to become a mother. Now though, having Dawson has been the best thing to ever happen to me. I didn't grow up in a loving home where my parents would cuddle me and tell me they loved me. My father was a drunk and loved to beat my mom, then he decided that when I turned thirteen it was my turn to cop the brunt of his anger.

"I know you don't, baby." I squeeze his little hands. "But, remember that I only have a half day today and then we are going away for the holidays." His little nose scrunches, I can see he is trying hard not to smile, so I tickle his sides and don't stop until he is squealing. Now that he is happy, I take the opportunity to get his shoes on and grab our things as we head out the door but then freeze the second I see the *Black Mamba Petunia* sitting there on the welcome mat. I look side to side before I reach down grab the freaking flower and shove it in the trash. I am so over this shit! If I had the money to move I would have done it months ago.

"Mama, what that?" I lock the door and grip Dawson's hand, heading for the school daycare.

"Just something someone dropped darling, nothing to worry about." I hate lying but I have no choice, he's four and wouldn't understand what's going on.

I hate leaving Dawson, especially when he cries for me and screams *Momma* as I turn and walk away. If I had another option and didn't have to go to school or work I wouldn't until he was at least school age but, unfortunately, I don't have the luxury of being rich. The walk to my first class is short. I'm still nervous about spending the holidays with Leah and her friends. I've met Cody and I know both the girls through Katie but I haven't met the others including her boyfriend, Darius. Leah tells me that they are all excited to meet me and have no issues with the fact I have a son. Honestly, it used to bother me that people would judge me simply because of my age and being a mom, now, I couldn't give a shit what they think. Dawson is the single most important person in my life and everything I do daily is for him and him alone.

Just as I'm taking my seat in class, my phone pings with a text. I pull it from my pocket and cringe, it's from Dawson's daycare. Being a single parent means I only have one income, some weeks when the diner doesn't have enough shifts and students cancel their tutoring sessions I'm left short and have to choose between rent, food, electricity and all the other shit. I haven't had any shifts at the diner for the past couple of weeks and thanks to the Christmas break, my tutoring sessions are next to none, which means I'm behind on rent and daycare. Well, I'm about a month behind on Dawson's daycare bill.

I swipe open the message, and a whoosh of air escapes me as I fight back tears.

> Miss Karver, with many attempts made to try and contact you in regards to the payment of your son's care with our center, and the account being overdue for the amount of $457.32 we have no choice but to terminate his spot here with our center. You will need to collect him immediately and organize payment within the next two weeks or we will have no choice but to take legal action. Kind regards, Jennifer Teal, Center Manager.

I close my eyes and fight back the tears that threaten to spill, no matter how hard I try I can never seem to get ahead. I'm here at CHU on a scholarship. I bust my ass every day at school and work as much as I can. I'm so thankful that on the nights I have to work, I have Jeff who watches Dawson for me. He has been a saint and is always there when I need him. Speaking of Jeff, he waltzes into class, shoots me a wide smile and comes to claim the seat next to me.

"Morning, beautiful." He hands me a Starbucks cup and I beam at him.

"Have I told you that you are amazing?" He chuckles as I take a sip of pure heaven. "You are way too good to me." He rolls his eyes playfully.

"How was my little man this morning?" Jeff is amazing but I don't like how he claims Dawson as his. I mean, I appreciate everything he does for us but that doesn't give him the right to act possessively over my son. I bite my tongue and force a smile, I won't allow this to bother me this morning.

"Not liking the fact he has to go to daycare," I say dejectedly. He shoots me a sympathetic look.

"If I didn't have school you know I would watch him." I smile my thanks and nod. "What are you and the little man doing over the break? I was thinking we could hang out and take Dawson to see some lights–"

I cut in before he can continue. "We're actually going away with some friends." A look of anger crosses his face before it's masked quickly, I swear if I wasn't paying such close attention I would have missed it.

"What friends?" Before I can answer the professor walks in effectively cutting our conversation off. I won't lie I am grateful for the interruption. I hate that Jeff makes me feel like I have to run everything by him first. He's a great guy and everything but he also comes off as overbearing and controlling. I know he means well and just cares about Dawson and me, but he also needs to remember he isn't my boyfriend and he isn't Dawson's father so we don't need his permission for anything.

I rush out of class and head straight for the daycare, I know it was reckless of me not to go straight to the center but I had to finish this exam or I would have failed. I have to maintain a certain grade or I risk my scholarship. I practically run the whole way there and cringe the moment I walk into the center to find Jennifer standing there with a stern look on her face. I screech to a stop breathless and try my best to keep the grimace off my face. I'm ashamed that I can't afford my own child's daycare bill.

"Miss Karver." The harsh tone of her voice and the way she looks down her nose at me grates on my nerves. "We were thirty minutes away from calling child services." My eyes widen, and I have to bite down on my tongue to keep my retort from bursting past my lips. "Dawson's enrolment has been revoked until the payment owed has been paid, with Christmas break we have agreed to grant you three weeks to pay in *full*." I grind my teeth and force myself to remain calm as I nod my understanding. I brush past her and head for Dawson's room and grab his bag before making my presence known. The moment he sees me a smile spreads across his face as he races across the room. I bend down, scoop him into my arms and hug him to me. I don't waste time as I leave the center, there is no way I can come up with that type of money in three weeks.

"Momma, we go way?" I push all my worries away as I focus on Dawson. I've tried so hard to make sure he has everything he needs but sometimes I fall short and I spend nights crying myself to sleep because of it.

"Yeah, baby, we just have to finish packing then we're leaving." He giggles in my hold and tries to clap as best he can. Seeing that smile on his face makes all of the day-to-day struggles worth it. I'll bust my ass every single day of my life just to make sure that smile remains on his face. As his mother it's my job to put his happiness before my own.

My arms are dead by the time we reach our apartment, Dawson is getting way too big for me to carry like this but I refuse to stop until I am physically unable to do it any longer. I cried when he refused to continue breastfeeding at eighteen months, that was hard for me as that was our bonding time. The sight of another *Black Mamba Petunia* has me halting a couple of feet away from my door. Fuck! This guy has gotten bold. Messages and phone calls are one thing but now that he knows where I live I don't feel safe anymore, but it's not like I have another option. I take a deep breath, place Dawson on his feet, then grab the freaking flower before he can touch it. Unlocking the door, I let him in first before I lock the door and throw the flower in the trash, praying that this one will be the last.

I spot Cody's car the second it rounds the corner. She pulls to the curb just in front of me. Leah leaps from the car to help me load our bags as I strap Dawson's car seat into the car, then him. I round the car and smile my thanks to Katie as she hops out to let me in to claim the middle seat.

"Let's roll!" Leah shouts excitedly. Just as we hit the interstate, Leah's phone begins to ring.

"Hey, you." Cody fake gags and I can't help but smile, I'm assuming from how her face lights up that it's her boyfriend Darius on the other end of the call. "Yeah, we're just hitting the interstate now." Leah told me that her boyfriend, brother, and a couple of their friends left yesterday but they had to stay back and finish their exams like me. "Uh, we're not fighting." She sounds utterly perplexed as she says that. "Agreed. I hated not waking up next to you." A pang of jealousy hits me—I wish I had that.

"I make ew better, Lee," Dawson calls out, my heart melts at how caring my boy is, and Leah shoots him a wink.

"Love you." Leah melts into her seat as she utters those words, ends the call and sighs.

"You two are so cute it makes me sick," Cody mocks.

"And seeing you and my brother together doesn't make me ill?" Cody just shrugs and shakes her head before saying.

"We're just... hanging out." I can hear the longing in

Cody's voice, something tells me her and Leah's brother are having trouble in paradise.

"Are you sure everyone doesn't mind spending the holidays with a random girl and her kid?" I ask, feeling like I'm intruding on their holiday and I know that they all must want to let loose and party. I don't want me and Dawson to hinder their fun.

"Of course not," Katie reprimands.

"They'll love it. Nathan is excited to finally get to meet you and Dawson," Leah says. "Plus, it will finally stop Darius from thinking I made you up."

"Why would he think you made me up?" I ask, slightly confused why her boyfriend would think that.

"Darius is jealous of the toilet paper for touching her hoo-ha," Cody mocks, earning an eye roll from Leah.

"What's hoo-ha, Mommy?" Dawson asks. I cringe, and Leah shoots me an apologetic look I wave her off.

"Nothing sweetie," I say as I places a kiss on his head. We spend the next few hours listening to music and singing along until Dawson falls asleep. Not wanting to wake to disturb him, we cut the music and fill the car with conversation. I ask Leah about her and Darius, and she tells me her story. It has me swooning and claiming that they have an epic love story. Katie and Cody fill me in on their friendly relationships with Crue, Saint and Corvin.

"What about you?" Leah asks me. I sigh and look over at my son with a sad smile.

"There isn't much to tell, I was sixteen and thought I was in love. He left, I found out eight weeks later I was pregnant. I tried to find him. I went to his house, only to find it vacant. He disappeared from my life and broke my heart." That's the version I tell people, except the truth is it was much more complicated.

"I'm so sorry," Leah whispers.

"It's okay. I mean, he may have vanished but he left me

behind the best gift I could have ever asked for. Dawson makes all the heartache worth it. I wouldn't change a thing." I mean it, I wouldn't change a single thing because all the shit I went through still led me to have the best kid in the world. We spend the rest of the drive talking aimlessly and getting to know each other better. Cody and Katie are amazing. I've known those two for a while but Leah is new to me. I can already tell her and I are going to get along just fine.

"Oh my God," I breathe out at the sight of the cabin in front of me. It's stunning and something you would see in a magazine.

"Right? It's so beautiful here. Just wait till the morning when you get to see the view, it is gorgeous," Katie says. Cody parks the car and the four of us all jump out to stretch. My back is aching and my legs are sore from sitting for so long, but the sight in front of me has made it all worth it. The air here is crisp, and the smell of pine surrounds us. I close my eyes and inhale a deep breath, loving being out here in nature without the fear of waking to another flower outside my door in the morning.

"Fuck, stop that!" I snap my gaze toward where Leah is currently wrapped up in her boyfriend's arms. I look toward the porch, and I know without a doubt that the guy standing there is Leah's brother Corvin, they look like carbon copies of each other. I reach in and carefully unbuckle Dawson and clutch him against me, trying not to wake him.

"Come on, let's grab your things." Leah leads the guys over to us and introduces me to Darius and Corvin. They both offer to carry mine and Dawson's bags so I only have to worry about my son. It's so nice to have help. I'm used to doing everything by myself and not having anyone to rely on.

"Where're the guys?' Cody asks as we walk up the path toward the cabin.

"They tried to wait up but they crashed. Katie your boys said to tell you to lock the basement door after yourself. Nathan took the fold-out bed in the theatre room so, Val, you and your boy can have the spare room next to Darius's." Leah darts in front of the guys and opens the door for them. The only light that is on is in the entryway. I would love to look around but I'm bone tired and just need sleep. Corvin hands Katie her bags, and she gives a shy wave before disappearing. Corvin blocks Leah from being able to climb the stairs. I stand behind her and feel slightly awkward until Cody comes to stand beside me.

"What's up?" she asks, Corvin smiles down at her with pride in his eyes.

"I know shit has been hard for you but I just wanted to say I am so fucking proud of you for finishing your English paper and not quitting. Also, Darius told me about Alaska." She tenses at the mention of her going to Alaska, she had told us about her decision in the car. "I spoke with Mom and Dad and told them about it, they agreed with me that this would be good for you."

"W-what?" she stutters out.

He smiles down at her. "I may not enjoy the sight of you and dickhead together." Darius snorts but doesn't comment. "But I also know he is a lot of the reason why you are doing so well. I expect your ass on a plane back to CHU to visit me every two months." She squeals then launches herself at her brother. He drops my bags to catch her. I smile at them, envious of the bond they have. I don't have any siblings so I don't know what it's like to have someone in your corner constantly.

"I love you, Corv."

"I love you too, Lee."

The moment they release each other, Darius leads me to

my room where he places my bags on the end of the bed. Leah tells me where the bathroom is and where her room is in case I need her. I smile my thanks and thank her again for letting me and Dawson come. She waves me off, promises to introduce me to everyone in the morning and give me a tour of the cabin and the grounds.

"Leah, go. I swear we will be fine," I say with a smile. She nibbles her bottom lip clearly feeling bad for leaving me when she shouldn't.

"Okay, if you need me I'm right next door." I nod, Darius smiles as he closes the door after Leah. After I get Dawson into bed, I strip down to my singlet and panties and slip in beside him. Drawing him close, I let his scent lull me to sleep.

CHAPTER FOUR

Valance

I awake to my little man peppering kisses all over my face. A smile breaks out across my face and my heart does a little flip at how freaking sweet he is. I spend the next few minutes tickling him and playing before I get him dressed and ready for the day. I gather my things for a shower, then pause as I look at Dawson who is sitting on the bed flicking through his book. Normally I would leave him and shower if we were at home, but we're on the second story and I'm scared that he may tumble down the stairs while I'm in the shower. Crap, I drop my clothes on the bed and pick Dawson up as I go next door to Leah's room. I knock twice and wait.

The moment the door opens and I see Leah smiling at me the words burst free. "Could I ask a favor?"

"Of course, Val. What do you need?" I feel fucking horrible that I have to ask this of her.

"Could you please watch him while I take a quick shower. I swear I won't be long. I'm just worried about the stairs if he came out of the room while I was in there and—" She cuts me off before I can continue rambling and making an even bigger fool out of myself in front of her and Darius.

"Val!" she snaps. "Go shower, wash your hair, do whatever you want, and take your time. Darius and I will take Dawson down and get him breakfast. Crue and Saint will love having the little guy to play with." My eyes widen in surprise.

"Are you sure?" She grabs Dawson from my hold and rests him on her hip before placing a hand on my shoulder and smiling kindly.

"Yes! Go shower, and take your time. When you're done, breakfast will be ready and waiting for you downstairs." I feel tears building and try to blink them away.

"Thank you, Leah."

"Val, we're all here for you. Once you get to know the guys you will understand that we are family and we take care of our own. You and Dawson are ours now. Whatever you need, we got you." Before the tears can fall I nod quickly and rush back to my room. I close the door and rest my head against it, feeling a sense of warmth wash over me. I've never had anyone to help me aside from Jeff, and I only ask for his help when I absolutely have to.

I do as Leah said and take my time in the shower. I can't remember the last time I was able to actually wash my hair properly, and to top it off I shaved as well! I haven't been able to complete both tasks in the shower at the same time since before Dawson was born. The shower head is freaking amazing and if it was detachable, my shower would have lasted significantly longer.

After changing and brushing my hair, I slip on my black yoga pants and slip my feet into my black Ugg boots before throwing on the off-the-shoulder cream sweater that I snagged for four dollars from the thrift store. Nothing I own is brand new, I can't afford it but I try to get all Dawson's clothes from Walmart when needed. His winter jacket is from the thrift store, I can't afford the thirty-dollar price tag for one of those at the store.

I drop my toiletries in my room before I finally make my way downstairs, nerves thrumming through my body. I'm worried that they won't like me and be salty that I've brought a kid into their rental for the holidays. I stop at the landing of the stairs and follow the sounds of laughter and conversation past the massive kitchen, it's gorgeous and I envy the owner of this place. The things I could cook in there. I shake away those thoughts and plaster a smile on my face. As I round the corner into the dining room, the smile vanishes at the sight of him.

My heart pumps double time inside my chest at the sight of him holding Dawson. "Get the hell away from my son!" The room falls silent at my outburst. Beckett's head snaps up and the moment his eyes collide with mine they widen a fraction.

"Valance…" he whispers my name. I rush forward and stop a foot away, I can feel the other's gazes on me but my sole focus is on the bastard who is holding my son.

"Give him to me now!" I grit out, hating that I can hear the hurt in my own voice. I never thought I would see him again, not after that night, and yet, here he sits with his friends in this lavish house, happy and without a care in the world. My anger peaks the longer I stare at him, his pale green eyes shine with confusion as he looks from Dawson to me.

"He's your… son?" Beck utters, barely above a whisper, *Shit.*

"Yes." I dart my gaze to Leah pleading silently for her to help me.

"Becky, pass me, Dawson," she says but Beck ignores her, keeping his gaze fixed on me.

"How old is he, Valance?" His tone is laced with anger. My shoulders bunch as I ball my hands into fists at my sides.

"He's... four." Beckett's brows jump to his hairline as his eyes widen. Dawson reaches for me and I lurch forward, yanking him from Beckett's hold, clutching him against my chest and peppering kisses on his head. I look to Leah hoping she can tell from the look in my eyes that I need her help now more than ever. "I need to go home." My words seem to be what snaps Beck out of his stunned state. He's on his feet and closes the space between us. I tighten my hold on Dawson and crane my neck back to meet his angry stare.

"You aren't taking *my* son anywhere!" he snarls. Gasps break out around the room.

"Fuck you, Beckett, he isn't yours!" A humorless laugh leaves him and I tense in preparation. Years may have passed but I know Beckett and that laugh means he is about to blow up at me.

"He isn't mine?" I nod stiffly. "Right, so, Valance, why the fuck did you name *your* son after me?" I shake my head unable to speak as fear grips me.

"Oh, shit," Darius mutters. "Beckett Dawson."

Fuck!

"Please, don't," I choke out, shaking my head and fighting back the tears that are so close to falling. Dawson wraps his arms around my neck, clearly feeling the tension in the room. I try to take a step back only for Beck to take one forward, telling me he will chase me down if I run.

"You gave *my* son my last name as his first name," he shouts. Dawson wails in fright. I try to calm him and rub soothing circles on his back but he won't quieten down. I need to find a way out of here now before Beckett tries anything stupid. "You're not taking him anywhere!"

"Screw you, Beckett, you'll never get near him," I growl.

"I'll take your ass to court. I have the money and you don't, so say your goodbyes now." Panic fills me, if what he says is true, and he does have the financial backing, I'd be fucked. There is no way I can afford a lawyer or court fees. I won't fucking let him take my son from me!

"Take me to court and I'll tell them how you are a murderer. You and I both know I have the proof of your crime." I keep my angry stare on Beckett but I hear the others climb to their feet, I'm out numbered. None of these people know me and I can already tell that nothing I say or do will sway them, they are loyal to the murderer that stands before me.

"You can try, but heed my warning, *Valance*," Darius spits my name like it burns his tongue. "You run your mouth to anyone and I promise you that we will bury you six feet fucking deep and take that kid from you without remorse if you try to keep him from Beck." Tears flow freely down my cheeks. I begin to feel the walls closing in on me. I look to Leah begging with my eyes for her help but I see it, in the depths of her green eyes, that she won't stand against Beckett. I'm on my own. Beckett darts forward and tears Dawson from my arms. He screams for me. I attempt to reach for him but my arms are gripped from either side and I'm being pulled from the room. Dawson turns to me with tears flowing down his cheeks, the look of fear in his eyes will haunt me for years to come.

"Momma!" He reaches for me and I try to fight with everything I have to get free, to get back to my son but their hold on me is strong and I'm too weak to fight them off.

"Please, Beckett, don't fucking do this!" I scream, the vacant look in his eyes scaring me. He doesn't react or blink as Dawson begins to slap his face screaming for me. He keeps his gaze on me as I'm dragged from the fucking room like a criminal.

CHAPTER FIVE

Beckett

It takes me a full three seconds after she has disappeared from the room to realize that Dawson is hitting me and scratching at my face as he screams for his mother. I look down at him unsure of what the fuck I am supposed to do. Five minutes ago, the kid looked at me like I was his favorite person and now, he looks at me with nothing but fear in his blue eyes–he has her eyes.

"Beck, let me take him," Leah says as she comes to stand in front of me. I clutch Dawson against my chest and pin her with a look daring her to take him from me. She doesn't protest or reprimand me she just smiles sadly. "He needs to be soothed, he's scared and wants his mother." Her words have my anger rising.

"He's mine!" I snarl. Darius stands by Leah and pins me with a look of warning.

"She's just trying to help, get him to stop crying or give him to someone who knows how to fucking make him stop." I try to cuddle him but he fights against me.

"Mommy, I want my momma!" he screams so fucking loud I flinch.

"Little man, want to come with me and get a cookie?" Leah says but Dawson isn't having it.

"I want momma!" he cries so hard he begins to gasp for air, fuck! Panic kicks in. Katie, Cody, and Saint round the table to stand in front of me as well, judging from the looks of the five of their faces they are clueless just like me.

"You need to take him to her, none of us know how to give CPR to a kid if he needs it." The sheer panic in Saint's voice mimics how I feel. I curse beneath my breath and push my way through them as I go in search of that lying bitch.

"Get the fuck off me, if you don't give me my son, I swear to Christ I'll fucking kill you!" I follow her shouts to the living room. Corvin and Crue have her pinned by her arms to the single seat, at the sound of Dawson's cries she snaps her gaze to me–him. "Dawson!" she shouts. He swings his head around toward her and cries harder at the sight of his mother. My hold on him tightens as she fights harder to get free. "Give him to me... please." Tears trek down her cheeks, and the sight fuels the anger inside me but the sounds of Dawson's cries are the only reason I give in. I place him on his feet and nod to Corv and Crue to release her. She slips from the seat and drops to her knees with her arms open as Dawson launches himself at her. He wraps his arms around her neck and tries his best to lock his legs around her waist. She buries her face in the crook of his neck and holds him tightly against her.

"Who is Val to you, Becky?" Leah whispers. It takes me a minute to think of how to explain who the fuck she is to me. I keep my gaze on Dawson and *her* as I answer.

"A part of my past I wish had stayed buried." Seeing her again causes memories of what I did to resurface. She fucking fled and I had no choice but to clean the fucking mess and run before she could turn me in. Valance lifts her tear-filled gaze to me, the anger and disgust I see in her eyes match exactly how I am feeling. The sight of her makes me sick, the knowledge that Dawson is–could be mine fuels the anger inside me to climb to new heights. I step down into the sunken living room. Valance tenses and quickly climbs to her feet awkwardly while still holding Dawson. His hold on her hasn't lessened, I feel like shit for scaring him. She's different but the same. I always knew Valance's beauty would only enhance as she got older and I wasn't wrong. Her auburn hair is longer now, her blue eyes filled with memories of a life lived. It's so strange standing here in front of my family looking at the girl who sold me the fuck out.

"I go home, Momma," Dawson cries out. She tenses for a second and darts her gaze around the room looking for an exit.

"Try it and you'll regret it," I say in a flat tone. She pins me with what I'm sure she is hoping is a glare that doesn't fool me. She is a fucking con artist.

"I know baby, maybe… we could get your toys from upstairs and you can play while… mommy talks to… Beckett?" I grit my teeth in annoyance, her eyes plead with me to allow her to do this.

"I'll go grab them. Where are they?" Saint asks. Valance purses her lips clearly wanting to deny him but she is smart enough to know this is her only choice.

"His books are on the bed. If you could bring his backpack down as well, that would be great." Saint nods and takes off to retrieve the shit she asked for while the rest of us stand here in tension-filled silence.

"Momma?" Dawson pulls back and stares at her, her features soften the second she looks at him.

"Yeah, baby?" she says with a smile that I can tell is forced.

"I go *pot-pot.*" Worry fills her features as she turns back to look at me. I keep my face blank of all emotion except my anger, I allow her to see that.

"He needs to go potty." I remain silent not giving a shit, that's a her problem not a me one.

"Fucking hell," I hear Cody grit out before she brushes past me. "Come on, I'll show you where it is." Valance smiles her thanks and moves to follow after Cody. Before she can take a single step past me, I grip her arm. Her gaze immediately snaps to mine, her eyes flick between mine searching for something.

"Don't try anything, you won't make it far," I warn. She sighs, then nods her understanding before I let her go. Dawson frowns up at me as they walk past me to follow Cody. Saint crashes into the room holding the shit she asked for. He drops it on the coffee table and my eyes zero in on the book. I stand here stunned and utterly fucking confused as to how that fucking book is sitting here right now.

"Do you want us to leave you or…" I can't peel my eyes off the book, I can't even form words to answer Corvin so I just shake my head as I reach down and grab it. It looks exactly the same as it did years ago. *Goosebumps*, the title brings a smile to my face.

"Dat mine!" I swing my head to the side to see Valance standing there with Dawson. Cody moves over to where Corvin sits on the recliner. Valance drops her gaze to my hands and her eyes widen.

"Shit!" I frown at the sound of panic in her voice. She rushes forward and tries to grab the book but I hold it out of her reach.

"Momma!" Dawson screams so fucking loud it has me cringing.

"Beckett, please give him the book!" I glare at her.

"Why the fuck should I?" I snap.

"It mine, it mine!" Dawson begins to cry and I can't for the fucking life of me understand why.

"It's his favorite book and no one is allowed to touch it, please give it to him." It takes me a solid minute to register what she is saying, when it all clicks into place I hand the book to the kid. He snatches it and clutches it against his chest before he buries his face in her neck again. She sags with relief.

"Why the fuck–" Before I can finish going off at her she cuts me off.

"Please stop cussing in front of him!" My brows jump to my hairline.

"Did she just use her mommy voice to tell Beck off?" I cut a look at Crue, that has him and Saint busting out into hysterics. Valance cringes and drops her gaze to the floor. She lowers herself to the ground and reaches out to grab the bag Saint got for her. She pulls out some cars and crayons and then reaches for the other coloring books Saint brought in. She turns Dawson in her hold and positions him between her legs so he can play. I want to fucking scream at her, call her all he names under the fucking sun but if he really is my son, I can't allow him to hear me speak to his mother like that, so instead I sit on the coffee table because I refuse to park my ass on the ground by her.

"Val?" Leah calls to her quietly, Valance takes a deep breath before she slowly turns to face Leah. "Can I get you something to eat or drink?" Valance shakes her head and scoffs.

"I'd rather not take anything from you unless it's a ride back to CHU." The anger in her voice can be heard around the room. Leah drops her gaze to her lap, and D wraps his arm around her shoulders and pulls her into his side.

"You want to be pissed off, fine, but you don't fucking speak to her like that!" Darius growls. Valance doesn't cower from the pressure of his gaze.

"And you don't get to butt in on anything to do with me or my son. Your girlfriend showed her true colors and made a choice to allow a child to be ripped from his mother!" she snaps back at Darius.

"Fuck it." Valance's eyes shoot wide as she stares down at Dawson in horror. "I fuck it, Momma." Her eyes slam shut and she shakes her head in defeat.

"That's my bad," Darius mutters. Valance waves him off and turns Dawson to face her, he smiles up at his mother.

"Munchkin, that is not a nice word and you shouldn't say that."

"Fuck, no good, Momma?" Saint and Crue can't contain their laughter. Valance shoots them a look that has them both clamping their mouths shut and sitting up straighter.

"No, it's a word only grown-ups can say." Dawson nods.

"I sowii, Momma." He gives her a hug and then goes back to playing with his toys. She looks at me expectantly waiting for me to say something.

"You say he isn't mine, yet my last name is his first name and he has my book." A whoosh of air escapes her.

"What do you want me to say, Beck?" She sounds defeated.

"The truth, Valance!" I snarl.

"Fine, his name isn't Dawson and he has your book because I gave it to him. You left it in my room the night you disappeared from my life, happy now?" There it is, the fire in her eyes I used to thrive off of.

"I didn't disappear, you left!" I snap. She opens her mouth to argue but I don't want to hear her lies so I push on. "What's his name then?" She nibbles on her bottom lip. I can tell she is debating on if she should be honest or not so I pin her with a look that promises pain if she lies.

"Fine, his name is Matthew." My eyes widen, and I feel the others gazes on me, they would have no idea that Matthew is my middle name. She holds my gaze as she continues. "His full name is Matthew Karver...Dawson." I fail to keep the shock from my face but I need to hear her say the words.

"Is he mine?"

CHAPTER SIX

Three simple words.

Three words that hold more weight than they should. His eyes dare me to lie but what's the point? Dawson is Beckett's twin, he looks so much like his father it hurts to look at him some days. I wrap my arms around my son and hold him tight as I answer the loaded question.

"Yes." I expect him to scream and shout, except, he does none of that, just smirks cruelly down at me.

"Enjoy your last holiday with him. He won't be going home with you." Tears cloud my vision, this man standing before me isn't the same guy I knew years ago. This man is hardened, jaded and angry at the world. The Beckett I once knew was kind, loving and wanted nothing more than to protect me from the monsters that I lived with. I carefully untangle myself from Dawson and step around so I stand in front of Beck, imploring him with my eyes to not do this.

"He's all I have, Beckett. I am begging you to not take him from me." A gasp escapes me when he snaps his arm out, grips the back of my neck and pulls me to him. I'm forced onto my tip toes as he bends down so we are eye level. I see nothing but hatred in his gaze as he looks at me and that cuts deep.

"I once begged you to not leave me and look what happened." He releases me with a hard shove. I stumble back a step, shocked to my core. Leah darts out in front of me facing Beck.

"Becky, you need to cool off," she says in my defense.

"She hid my kid!" he roars. Dawson shrieks in fright.

"And you are hurting the mother of your child in front of him! He doesn't need to see that crap. Take a walk and calm down." Dawson begins to cry and I rush over to him plucking from the ground and holding him against me to try to calm him, he's never been around this type of tension or raised voices before. Beckett shoots me a glare before storming out of the room. Darius and Corvin both go after him. The second the front door slams closed, I gather Dawson's things and race from the room, taking the stairs as quickly as I can with Dawson in my hold.

I kick the door shut behind me and groan when I see there is no lock!

"Great," I bite out as I drop the bag and place Dawson on the bed. He sniffles and uses the backs of his hands to wipe his tears away. I race around the room and gather all our things, I don't know how the hell I am going to afford an Uber from here and especially with it being Christmas Eve but I don't have a choice, I need to get the hell out of here.

I lay here next to Dawson as he naps with my arms banded around him. It's early afternoon when a knock sounds at the door. I debate ignoring it but when they knock again and Dawson stirs. I decide it's better to leave him to nap rather than wake him and have him be grumpy. I slip from the bed carefully and quietly tiptoe over to the door and open it. I frown when I see Corvin standing there. I slip out of the room and quietly close the door behind myself. We stand here awkwardly for a minute as he rubs the back of his neck and shoots me an awkward smile.

"I know this is fucked up and everything–"

"You think?" I snap, his eyes soften as he drops his arm back to his side.

"Look, I know you're pissed at everyone and I don't know the story behind you and Beck but I do know him. Whatever happened between the two of you must have been bad for him to leave someone he cares about." I drop my gaze to the floor unable to handle the judgment in his eyes. "Valance?"

I slowly lift my gaze back to his. "I won't tell his story," I whisper.

"I respect that but that wasn't what I was going to say. Firstly, I want to say I'm sorry about earlier. I never should have dragged you away from your kid." I frown.

"Oh…" I'm not really sure how I should answer that. Am I pissed that he did that? Yes! But I also understand that Beckett is his friend and of course, he would believe him over me, so I can't really be too angry at him.

"Look, we have a tree and thought the little guy would like to decorate it and bake some cookies and shit with us?" My eyes widen in surprise but then I think of Beckett and his threat.

"That's really sweet of you but–"

He cuts me off. "I won't let him take the kid from you, Valance." The conviction in his tone has me stunned silent. "I'm no saint but I also know that every kid needs their mom. You have my word that I will not let that happen, but you do need to sort shit with Beckett." I blow out a frustrated breath and nod.

It's not like I have much choice, I get no cell service here so I couldn't even call an Uber or Jeff to see if he could pick us up. "I have a couple of little things for Dawson in the morning, can I put them under the tree?"

Corvin beams at me and nods. "Of course, you can, we have a hot tub out back that he can play in tonight as well." I shake my head.

"Dawson can't swim!" I say in a panic. He reaches out and places a hand on my shoulder, and smiles reassuringly.

"That's why he has uncles and aunts that will watch over him." Corvin may not understand it but his words mean more than he will ever know. I never thought Dawson would have a family that would band around him and care for his wellbeing. The situation between Beck and I is shit but something inside me is screaming that I can trust Corvin.

"Okay," I whisper.

"Where is the little guy, can I take him down?" I'm about to tell him that he's napping when the door opens to reveal a yawing little boy that melts my heart. Corvin drops down onto one knee in front of Dawson who is still half asleep. "Hi, my dude, I'm your uncle Corv." I cover my mouth with my hand and fight back tears. Dawson smiles shyly at Corvin.

"Hi, I Dawson." I smile behind my hand.

"Well, little dude, we have a Christmas tree downstairs that needs to be decorated for Santa, do ya think you can help us?" Dawson jumps up and down and claps excitedly.

"Momma, I go uncool Corbin?" I fight my laughter from slipping free at the way he says *uncool*, Corvin doesn't seem to mind that he can't say his name which is sweet. I pretend to ponder his question for a second.

"Promise to be good and use your listening ears?" He nods eagerly.

"Well, I guess so then," I say. Dawson squeals in delight before launching himself at Corvin. He catches him with ease and stands with my boy in his arms.

"I think your momma needs to help, don't you, little dude?" Before I can decline his offer, Dawson shouts.

"Yes, Momma helps too." Corvin grins triumphantly and winks. I sigh before following him back downstairs into the living room where the fire is going. I frown when I notice that tree is by the open fire. Everyone is gathered around, waiting for Dawson. I move to stand by the fire and keep my gaze focused on the floor not wanting to look at the others.

"Too good to sit with us, huh?" I snap my head up to see Beckett standing in the middle of the living room with an angry look on his face. Corvin and the others are sitting on the ground with Dawson opening decoration boxes.

I harden my stare and shake my head. "No, Beckett. I'm standing here because there is a fire behind me and in case you haven't noticed I have a four-year-old." His jaw locks for a second.

"How could I forget!" he snaps.

"Yo, enough," Corvin growls at Beck, before turning to look at me from his spot on the floor. "We lit the fire so it wasn't cold for the little dude." Corvin sounds genuinely confused and I feel like a bitch now.

"I appreciate that, I really do–"

"But?" Beckett cuts in. I cut my stare to him as I finish.

"It's an open fire! Kids and fires don't mix, Beckett, so no, I wasn't standing here because I think I'm better than anyone, I'm standing here so Dawson doesn't get burnt." His eyes widen as he curses under his breath. The other four guys jump to their feet and look at me with worried expressions on their faces. I take a step back suddenly feeling afraid with all their attention on me.

"What do we do?" Saint asks me and I frown. "About the fire." I stare at him in surprise.

"Uh…" I'm lost for words.

"We'll put the heat on and douse the fire, then move the tree to the games room," Corvin says.

"Yeah, we can carry it through the kitchen," Darius tacks on.

"Where are the buckets?" Crue asks, before they can continue rearranging everything to suit Dawson I cut in.

"Stop!" Everyone turns to face me, even the girls. "The fire is fine, do you have a screen?" The guys all exchange looks clearly not knowing what I'm talking about. Katie jumps to her feet drawing my attention to her.

"Yeah, there's one in the basement. Crue, Saint, come help me." I smile thanks as she leads the guys from the room. Beck walks over to me and I tense in anticipation, while the others go back to helping Dawson open up the boxes. We stand here shoulder to shoulder with a foot of space between us as we watch the others. Darius sits behind Leah with his arms wrapped around her waist, and Cody and Corvin keep a foot of space between them as they sit there and smile at my little man. Seeing him smile melts me every time, his happiness is the most important thing in the world to me.

"Why do you call him Dawson?" His voice has an edge to it, I keep my gaze focused on the others as I answer Beck.

"*He* is the one who demanded to be called Dawson, not Matthew," I answer honestly.

"Why?" I take a deep breath and decide to be honest. He deserves to know the truth about his son. I turn and look up at him to find his gaze is already on me.

"He asked me why our last names were different. I told him that Dawson was his daddy's last name and ever since that day he demanded to be called Dawson." Beckett's brows draw in as he frowns down at me, clearly not sure if he should trust my word or not. The stare-off between us is broken when Saint and Crue come into the room carrying a screen for the fire. I smile and thank them as they set it up around the fire. Saint and Crue head back to Katie and drop down onto the couch on either side of her. I furrow my brow trying to work out how the three of them fit.

"I won't let you leave with him." The conviction in his voice has me steeling my spine.

"I won't let him go, Beckett. Hate me all you want but my son stays with me." He reaches out, and grips my chin, turning me to face him. The look in his eyes steals my breath, his eyes daring me to challenge him. He should know me well enough to know I never do as I'm told.

"*Ours!*" I scrunch my face in confusion. "He's our son, Valance." Hearing those words come from his mouth has all the air whooshing out of my lungs and tears stinging the backs of my eyes. I flick my eyes between his and see nothing but sincerity. "I won't allow you to take him from me."

CHAPTER SEVEN

Beckett

I've been standing here strangling the fuck out of my beer for the past hour. Corvin, the prick, thought it would be a great idea to get everyone in the hot tub. It was, until Valance walked out in a fucking one piece that has more holes in it than the fucking holy Bible. I can tell she is uncomfortable in her own skin now, the girl shouldn't be. Having a child didn't diminish her beauty it only enhanced it. She's filled out in all the right places, her ass is bigger and each time she walks past it's like it has a sign stapled to it saying *spank me.*

"What was it you once said to me?" I don't move my head but peer at Darius out of the corner of my eye as he rests his forearms on the counter next to me. "Oh, that's it! If you glare any harder your face will crack." I narrow my eyes at the smart fuck. He throws his head back and laughs, forcing me to grip my bottle tighter or risk strangling his dumb ass. Ignoring him I focus back on the others outside. Leah, Katie, Cody, Corvin, Valance, Saint, and Crue all clap and cheer as Dawson jumps from Corvin's arms and paddles across to his mother. "He looks like you," Darius says quietly.

A whoosh of air escapes me. "I didn't even know I had a

fucking kid, Darius. She kept him from me for four fucking years!" The bitterness that coats my tone is hard to miss. The sight of her makes me sick, I want to punish her and make her fucking hurt as I did all those years ago! The person I fucking trusted most in this world betrayed me!

"From the sounds of things, she wasn't the only one who kept shit hidden." I flick my gaze to him and raise a brow prompting him to explain further. "Was she talking out of her ass when she said you murdered someone?" I drop my gaze instantly and nibble on my lip debating on if I should tell him. If I do, that means he's implicated in this as well.

"There is some truth to it." This is the only answer I can give him. I refuse to bring him down with me if Valance does decide to out me after all these years.

"I'll settle with that answer for now. What are you going to do, Beck? You can't lock her up and force her to stay." I lull my head to the side and shoot him a sly smirk.

"Says who?" I reply smugly. Darius rolls his eyes and shoots me a crooked smile. Our attention is drawn back to the others as Valance stands and hops out of the hot tub in that fucking suit that has holes everywhere. I don't miss the way Corvin's eyes linger on her ass and that shit grates on my nerves. He passes her Dawson who latches onto his mother. Leah leaps out of the tub and rushes over to get them some towels. Val eyes her warily for a second before thanking her and heading inside. Darius and I don't move when she pushes the back door open and rushes in shivering. She tries to wrap the towel around Dawson to keep him warm but he won't let go of her.

"Munchkin, I need you to hop down so I can wrap you up," she pleads.

"You carry me," he argues. Val closes her eyes for a second and takes a calming breath just as Leah walks in behind her.

"Can I help?" Leah offers. Val shakes her head.

"Thanks, but he won't go to you when he's this tired." Tired of watching this exchange like a bystander, I step out from behind the counter. Val's eyes widen at the sight of me but she says nothing when I step up beside her so Dawson can see me.

"If you let me wrap you up in your towel and get you changed, I'll help you set out some milk and cookies for Santa." Dawson's face lights up with a smile.

"Yes! I go Becky now, Momma." He practically flings himself at me, which in turn throws Val off balance and she stumbles into me. Dawson is sandwiched between us as I grip her waist to keep her steady. Her eyes snap to mine in fright, causing me to drop my hold like she burnt me. I snatch the towel from her hand and wrap it around Dawson like he's a burrito. Val stands there staring until I raise a single brow.

"We gonna stand here all night?" I snap. She shakes her head and quickly wraps the other towel around her body and leads the way to her room.

"The sexual tension between them has me hot and needy," I hear Leah say just before we hit the base of the stairs. She pauses outside her bedroom door and lowers her head. I give her a minute to gather her fucking shit but when she still doesn't open the door, I'm forced to make her.

"Open it, Valance, our son is cold." She nods her head robotically and pushes the door open. I follow after her and watch as she flicks the light on and rushes to the corner of the room where her bags are. She rummages through the duffle and pulls out a woolen worn onesie that even has the feet sock things on it. She grabs some other shit and places it on the bed. I eye the Pamper she has laid out before turning back to her. "Why is he wearing Pampers?"

She drops her gaze to the ground and scuffs her foot along the floor as she answers. "I didn't want him to have an accident and ruin the mattress. I... I can't afford the cleaning bill so this was easier."

I narrow my eyes. "Does he need to wear them?" She shakes her head. I reach out, grab the Pamper and chuck it to the side of the room. Dawson claps and cheers while Val stares up at me with her mouth open in shock.

"Beckett!" she growls in annoyance.

"I don't give a fuck about the mattress. He doesn't wear those fucking things again. Now, help me dress him." She nods stiffly, clearly taken aback by the demand but does as I ask. Once Dawson is changed she brushes his hair with a comb and rubs his face with some moisturizer then stands and looks at me awkwardly. I refuse to ask what her problem is, so I wait for her to speak but then her phone begins to ring next to Dawson on the bed. Before she can reach for it the clever little boy grabs it, swipes the screen, and answers the Facetime call.

"Hey, my man." I stiffen at the sound of a guy's voice before cutting my gaze back to Valance, who doesn't seem to notice the tension has just risen in the room.

"Hi," Dawson says.

"How are you, *my* boy." I clench my hands into fists at my side as I glare at the bitch I pro-created with. She purses her lips as she stares down at Dawson.

"I good. Me make cookies for Santa with Becky." There's a pause on the other end of the end for a brief second before the fucker speaks again.

"Aww, that's nice of your momma's friend to do that. Is this Becky girl nice?" Before Dawson can answer Valance takes her phone from him. "Hey, beautiful," the bastard says the moment he sees her.

"Hey, sorry now isn't a really good time can I call you after I put Dawson to bed?" she says.

"Yeah, of course. Give him a kiss for me." She nods before ending the call and turning to face me. Her eyes widen when she takes in the look on my face.

"How the fuck did you get service out here?" I grit out

through clenched teeth.

"Katie did something to my phone so I could use it." Fucking Katie is going to pay for that. I reach out and snatch her phone from her grasp. "Hey, give that back," she snaps as she rushes me. Before she can make a grab for her phone, I have my hand around her throat and spin us around so my back is to Dawson and he can't see what I'm doing to his mother. Her eyes widen in fear when I shove her against the closed door and tighten my hold on her neck.

I get right in her face as I speak low enough so Dawson can't hear. "You don't fucking talk to your bitch boy in *my* house and the next time I hear that cunt calling *my* son his boy, I'll snap his fucking neck." Her mouth drops open. I don't wait for a reply as I push back from her and turn to face Dawson who is staring up at me with a frown. I smile trying to ease his worry. "Want to help me with those cookies?"

"Momma come?" I fight the urge to deny him. Valance steps out from behind me and smiles down at him.

"I'll just get changed and then we'll head down." Dawson beams at her. I fucking hate that my own kid is terrified to be near me.

I fucking hate her.

Dawson places the tray with the cookies and milk on the small table we put next to the tree for him, then turns to us and claps. It brings a smile to my face to see him happy. It's strange, I may have just found out he's my kid but I can already tell I would do anything in this world to make sure he is happy and has the best fucking life. I'll never let him go through the struggles that I did. Valance, Katie, Saint and Crue all sit down on the carpet and play with Dawson as I lean against the wall and just watch.

"I can't believe he's yours," Leah says quietly from beside

me. She rests her head against my shoulder, so I shift my arm and wrap it around her as I draw her into my side. No one, not even Darius, understands the bond that Leah and I share. It's not sexual or anything like that, it's deeper. We connect on a level that I have never connected with anyone else before. Yes, we have fucked and it was fucking epic but it will never happen again because we both know that we aren't attracted to each in that way now. Plus, Darius will never let that shit happen again.

"Same," I answer honestly as she rests her head against my chest and wraps her arms around my waist. Valance chooses that moment to look over and at the sight of Leah and me, she frowns for a brief second before tearing her gaze away and forcing a smile as Dawson says something to her.

"What are you going to do, Becky?" she whispers. I keep my eyes on my son as I answer.

"She hid him from me, Lee. He has gone four years without a father because of her choices. I fucking hate her and if I could get rid of her and keep my kid, I would."

"He loves her, B, and he needs his mother. Even if you hate her, you have to find a way to work things out with her for his sake. She… needs your help." I frown and push her back. She drops her gaze to the floor and that pisses me off, so cup her face and lift it until she meets my gaze.

"What does that mean?" I ask quietly as I search her gaze for an answer. She reaches up and grips my wrists in her hold as Darius rounds the corner and comes to a halt at the sight of us. I ignore his presence needing to hear her answer more than I need to draw in my next breath.

"I think she is struggling financially–"

Leah is cut off before she can finish telling me what I want to know. "That is none of your business!" Valance snaps from beside us. Leah yanks free of my hold and stares at her friend with wide eyes. Valance has a murderous look on her face as she stands there with Dawson in her arms. He looks like he's ready to crash. Darius pushes forward and wraps his arm around Leah drawing her into his side.

"Val, I wasn't trying to overstep–" Valance scoffs forcing Leah to clamp her mouth closed.

"Yeah, you were. You don't know anything about me, Leah. You have no right to assume or speak on behalf about matters that don't concern you!" I growl as I step in front of Leah blocking Val's view of her, we stand here glaring at each other.

"She has every right to speak–" I start but the little bitch cuts me off!

"Well, the next time one of your bed warmers speaks to me about my kid, I'll make sure I listen to every word," she snaps mockingly before turning to leave. She makes it two steps before Darius is in front of her. I don't know why but I push forward ready to stop him if he tries anything with her. I frown at my actions and the fact protecting Valance came so naturally without even having to think about it. The look on Darius's face is murderous, his brown eyes shine with hatred as he scowls down at Val.

"You want to lash out at Beck, then have at it, but the next time you come at my girl or insinuate that there is shit happening between them when there isn't, you and I are gonna have fucking problems, feel me?"

Valance doesn't cower or drop her gaze as she answers. "Oh, then I look forward to sparring with you because I won't roll over and allow any of you to walk all over me and try to take my son away." She doesn't stick around for a reply, brushing past Darius as she heads up the stairs. I see it the way her shoulders droop as she climbs the stairs, she feels like a bitch for having a go at Leah. Valance is taking her anger out on Leah because she thinks her friend betrayed her. D cuts his gaze to me and raises a brow.

"Handle that shit now. I'm not gonna let your baby momma drama affect me and make me see things between you and my girl that isn't there." I hear his warning loud and clear. Darius is a jealous fucker and already hates how close Leah and me are. Val putting shit in his head will drive a wedge between me and him, and I won't fucking allow that to happen.

CHAPTER EIGHT

Just as I lay Dawson down and pull the covers up, the bedroom door bursts open. Beck opens his mouth to no doubt shout at me but I launch across the room and slap my hand over his mouth.

"Shh, he's asleep." When his eyes narrow, my eyes widen when I realize what I just did. I drop my hand and take a step back. "I'm sorry," I whisper. His brows draw in as he shoots me a filthy look before turning back to Dawson. The sight of him has all the anger draining from his features and a ghost of a smile tugging at the corner of his mouth. He steps around me heading for Dawson and on instinct, I follow his movements until he sits down on the edge of the bed and reaches out to run his fingers through our son's hair. The site has a lump forming in my throat. I never thought I would ever see Beckett again, which in turn meant Dawson would never meet his father. I lived with that guilt every single freaking day, but standing here and seeing the way Beckett looks at our boy, has a strange feeling blooming inside me.

"I want to know everything about him, Valance, every single detail!" he whispers. I hear the undertone of hurt that laces each of his words. I don't know what to say, so I just remain silent as guilt consumes me. I shouldn't feel bad but I do. I never intended for Beckett to not be a part of Dawson's life but by the time I found out I was even pregnant, he was gone from my life. He leans forward and places the softest kiss on Dawson's forehead before slowly climbing to his feet and looking down at me. "You've had every first with him. Tomorrow, that changes."

"What do you mean?"

"From now on, I'm a part of everything to do with him. Every holiday, special occasion, fuck, anything to do with him. I am going to be a part of it and I don't give a fuck if you don't like it."

I stare at him utterly thrown for a second before I gather myself. "I never tried to stop you, Beckett." Dawson stirs at the sound of my raised voice. I motion for Beckett to follow me out of the room, which he does and shuts the door quietly behind us as I move toward the banister.

"Continue on with your bullshit," he rasps out, earning a scowl from me.

"It's not bullshit, it's the fucking truth!" It all happens so fast. His hand is around my throat and then I'm pushed against the banister with my back arched over it. I grip his shirt in an attempt to hold on so he doesn't throw me over the edge.

"You fucking hid him from me, Valance," he shouts.

"Let me up!" I cry but he's too lost in his anger to see reason right now.

"You think you get to dictate what the fuck happens with *my* son?" I hear footsteps pounding up the stairs, but I don't dare take my eyes off him.

"He isn't just yours! I never hid him from you, Beckett. I tried to find you after that night but you were gone!" I scream.

"You fucking left me!" he shouts so loud I fear it will wake Dawson, who sleeps mere feet away.

"Beck, let her up, man." I think it's Corvin that says that but neither of us take our eyes off the other.

"I never left you, Beckett. My mother dragged me to the car and tried to leave town. I jumped out of the moving fucking vehicle, broke my ankle and limped all the fucking way home praying you would be there, but you weren't!" His face contorts in pain as he steps back and releases his hold on me. My anger is peaked and I'm not ready to stop lashing out. "I had no one. My father was dead, my mom ran off and I was on my fucking own." I spy Corvin, Darius, Leah and Crue out of the corner of my eye but I can't stop the words from spewing out of me. "I was alone, Beckett, everyone had left me. I had nothing and still when I found out eight weeks after you left that I was pregnant, I wasn't even mad because I had a part of you with me!" Tears trail down my cheeks as emotions I have fought for years to keep buried surface. "I raised *our* son on my own. I had no fucking help or even a place to call home. We went from shelter to shelter as I tried to finish school and busted my ass to earn a scholarship at CHU so I could make a better life for him and give our fucking son what we never had!"

My breaths are coming in rapid pants, tears flow freely but I don't care. He has done nothing but judge me and none of this is my fault. He ran the night he killed my father and I never heard from him again. I've struggled every single day since that night but I have never once blamed him for that. All I had hoped for was that he was happy and okay.

"You looked for me?" he asks quietly. I grit my teeth and clench my fists at my sides.

"I gave up trying to find you the day Dawson was born. I didn't have the luxury of hoping for you to come back after that day. You ran and never once worried about what you left behind. Newsflash, asshole, you left your fucking kid behind!" I scream as I shoulder past him and march into my room. I close the door and sigh when I see Dawson is still fast asleep. I lean against the door and slide down to my ass and cry. Beck was the boy who could always make me smile and make my darkest days brighter. Now, he is the man who forces the smile from my face and dampens my happiness.

After an hour of feeling sorry for myself and crying, I wipe my face and force myself to my feet so I can place the four presents I managed to get Dawson under the tree. I quietly tiptoe down the stairs so I don't wake the others, but the moment I round the corner and see the kitchen light on I freeze at the sight of all five guys leaning against the counter with a beer each in their hands. I don't have the energy to fight with him again so I head for the living room and slam to a stop at the sight of the mountains of presents beneath the tree. Shame washes over me at the sight of them. I look down at the four tiny presents in my arms and fight the urge to cry again.

"Most of those are for him." I turn to the side to see Saint standing next to me. He shoots me a kind smile.

"I don't understand," I whisper. Corvin and Crue come to stand on my other side while Beck and Darius stand next to Saint.

"When we left, we thought we would hit the mall a couple of hours away from here and kill time for Beck to calm down," Corvin says. "Then we realized, we have a nephew and none of us had brought him a gift, so we went shopping." He shrugs his shoulders like what they did isn't a big deal. They have no idea that for the past four years I have wished I would be able to give Dawson all of this, but I could never afford it. I drop my gaze to the floor, feeling embarrassed that they can do all of this and all I can manage is a measly four gifts.

"Thanks," I mutter as I turn to walk away. I make it two steps before Darius is blocking my exit from the sunken in living room.

"Aren't you going to put your presents under the tree?" I stare up at Darius wanting to smack the guy. He is out of his mind if he thinks I'm going to place my gifts under there!

"No, I'll just... give them to him when he wakes up," I grind out.

"Why?" Who the hell does Darius think he is to question me?

"Because I don't want to put them under the tree," I snap.

Darius eyes me warily for a second before he asks, "Why not?"

Having had enough of this shit and just bone tired from the exhausting day I decide to tell the truth. "Because my gifts are from the *on sale* rack while yours aren't. I had to save for weeks to afford four things for my son and yet you guys can fill half the room with gifts in a couple of hours." Darius's face drops. I hear the others cursing behind me. "I wish I could give him what is under that tree but I can't," I whisper, dropping my gaze yet again to the floor in shame and guilt that I can't give my own child more than second hand clothes or on sale toys.

I'm shocked to my core when arms grip my shoulders and turns me. I stare up at Beckett in surprise, his eyes are filled with anger but it's not directed at... me. "Every fucking thing under that tree is from *us*, every single one of us! From now on anything you need for Dawson, you tell me and I'll get it."

Frowning up at him I shake my head. "No." His brows jump to his hairline at my response.

"The fuck do you mean, *no*?" I pull out of his hold and step back. How the hell can he not get it?

"I will not allow you to throw money around and think it

fixes everything! Money may be great and make life easy, Beckett, but I don't expect you to cover everything for him. I'm fine paying for everything like I always have." I snort before adding on. "I mean, unless you're a millionaire, then sure you can pay for everything including a car to drive him to daycare." A light chuckle leaves me but when I see no one else laughs, I snap my mouth closed and look over at each of them. None of them will look at me. Crue seems to find the vaulted ceiling so interesting, Saint is staring at his shoes, Corvin just looks everywhere but at me, and Darius just stares at his hands, so I turn back to Beckett. The way his eyes bore into mine and hold a serious look has my mouth dropping open and my eyes widening. "Oh my God, you are a millionaire, aren't you?" I breathe out.

"No, of course not." I sigh in relief at Saint's answer.

"We're closer to billionaires," Crue tacks on, stealing the breath from my lungs and causing me to choke on my own spit. I slowly turn my gaze back to Beckett, who stands there with a blank look on his face. Oh my God, it hits me then.

"You didn't rent this cabin, did you?" I say barely above a whisper. He stuffs his hands in his pockets, straightens and stares down at me with a look that holds a challenge.

"Guess you weren't the only one harboring a secret, huh?" I blow out a loud exhale at his jab, not wanting to draw out this awkward encounter I weave my way through them and place the small gifts under the tree before turning back to face them standing there shoulder to shoulder in a united front. I run my gaze over each of them and without them needing to say a single word, I see the unwavering loyalty they have for each other in their gazes. It's awe inspiring to see. I've never had a friendship like they share well, I've never really had a friend until I met Jeff.

"Dawson and I won't be staying for the New Year, I made plans with a friend," I say before quickly making my exit. I hear the others grunting as they hold Beck back.

"Calm down."

"Let her go."

"Beck, stop," the guys all say as they try to calm their friend while I make my escape. I make it to the bottom of the stairs before I hear him finally speak.

"She won't get away from me a second time and she sure as fuck isn't taking my kid from me, *again*."

CHAPTER NINE

Beckett

Christmas day was a day I'll never forget for the rest of my life. Seeing how wide my kid's eyes went at the sight of all the presents under the tree had my chest filling with a sense of pride. He loved every single gift and made sure to rush around the room and hug each of us telling us it was the best Christmas ever. I watched Valance as he opened each gift. She forced a smile every time Dawson would show her what he got and fake being happy. When he got to her gifts though, his whole face lit up like the fourth of July. She bought him a train set, books, a jacket and a picture of the two of them at some park. Thousands of dollars' worth of gifts and his favorite one was the picture of him and his mother.

"You ready?" I shake my head to clear my thoughts and look over at Corvin as I nod. I follow him outside as Saint sets the alarm and locks the front door. I head for my car and freeze when I see Valance about to put Dawson in the back of Cody's car. Gritting my teeth, I march over to her and grip her arm, she snaps her gaze to me in fright.

"What's wrong?" she asks, clearly not picking up what the fuck I'm putting down.

"Get your shit, you two ride with me." Her brows raise

but I don't have time for her shit. I pluck Dawson from her hold and make my way over to my Audi, leaving her to get their shit. We were supposed to be here for another week but little miss I-think-I-have-control over there wouldn't shut the fuck up about plans for the New Year, so we're all heading back to CHU a week earlier than planned.

"I go Becky car?" I smile at my boy as I open the back door for Valance so she can strap the seat thing in.

"Yeah, little man, you ride home with me," I answer. Once she has the seat thing strapped in, I hand him to her as I walk over to Corv, Darius, Saint and Crue. "We good?"

A frown mars Corv's face as he looks over to Cody's car and watches her and Nathan slip inside. Honestly, I forgot Nathan was even here. I haven't seen much of him. "Yeah, Leah will ride with D and Crue, Saint and Katie are with me, so that leaves you, your boy and your girl alone in a car for eight hours." I narrow my eyes at Corvin and grind my teeth when Saint and Crue begin to cackle like girls.

"Coming from the guy with a face like a smacked ass at the sight of *his* girl riding with Nathan?" I snark. Corvin glares and flips me off before marching over to his vehicle.

"Ease up on him." I look to Darius to see him staring after Corvin with a worried look in his eyes.

"What's up with him?" I ask. D sighs and runs a hand through his before he answers me.

"Remember Lana?" I wrack my brain for a second trying to recall who she is.

"Corv's bitch ass ex that fucked with his head?" Saint asks. D nods and that's when I remember who she is. That fucking crazy ass bitch fucked with Corvin's head bad. She cheated on him and made him believe it was his fault because he was always at practice and she was lonely.

"Yeah, well, Cody may have seen some texts between him and her and called off... whatever the fuck was happening between them."

"Seriously?" Crue quips. Darius nods but I can see in his brown eyes he doesn't agree with Corvin's actions.

"Halfback, get your ass over here so I can cuddle into you." Darius smiles over at Leah as she rests against his bike. We do our bro shake before we all get in ours–well, except for Darius who has to ride back in this fucking cold ass weather with Leah. Corvin takes the lead, Cody follows after him and I hang back to let Darius and Leah in front of me, leaving me to take up the end of our little train. Valance and I haven't spoken a single word to each other since Christmas two days ago. Every time I'm around her all I want to do is strangle the shit out of her.

We're about two hours into our trip of awkward silence when Dawson begins to cry. I flick my gaze up to check him in the rearview mirror as Valance leans around her seat to check on him.

"What's wrong, munchkin?" Her and I may not have spoken a word to each other but Dawson has filled the silence with singing or talking to his mother and me.

"I… my bibby… there." I frown and look over at Valance. She curses under her breath then unclips her belt and leans over the console to reach into the back. Her ass is right in line with my face and distracting the fuck out of me so, I slap her perky ass and relish in the squeal that tears from her.

"Here you go." I fight the smirk from breaking free at her breathy tone. She slips back into her seat and shoots me a glare that I ignore as I look in the mirror to see Dawson clutching a weathered looking blanket. "Every kid has something that soothes them, Dawson's is his *bibby*." I nod even though I have no fucking idea what that means, all the Google searches I did never mentioned anything about a comforter. It takes him mere minutes before his eyes close and he passes out. The sight of him sleeping in the back of my Audi is something I thought I would never see but I'm not mad about it.

Another hour of silence passes and the tension in the car only seems to grow. Valance has been fidgeting and shifting in her seat every few minutes. Silence has never bothered me, I never found the need to fill it with needless chit chat but I know she hates it, she always has. I mentally berate myself for allowing thoughts of the past to crawl to the surface inside me. I may have known who she was years ago but this woman sitting beside me is a foreign being. The girl I knew would never have hid my kid. She may have spun a good story last night but that doesn't mean I believe her lying ass. I plan to ask our resident hacker—aka Katie–to look into her story and see if it holds any merit as soon as we are back home.

"The girls mentioned that you're leaving soon?" I white knuckle the steering wheel and make a mental note to *speak* with said fucking girls.

"What else did your little friends tell you?" I grit out. She drops her gaze to her lap and nibbles on that fucking bottom lip. It always drove me crazy when she did that and clearly that fact still hasn't changed.

"Just that you leave after the New Year and will be gone for six months." I look over at her when I hear a hint of fear in her voice. What the fuck is she hiding?

"I would have thought you would have been celebrating that I'd be out of your life again." A whoosh of air escapes her and her shoulders hunch in defeat.

"Beck, I know you hate me–"

"I don't hate you." She swings her gaze to me her mouth slightly ajar. I look at her as I deliver the final blow. "I just can't stand the fucking sight of you. If he wasn't so attached to you, I would have thrown your ass to the curb and raised him without you." Her eyes widen but she says nothing as she turns to peer out her window. Silence ensues for hours, we're an hour out from CHU when I check the time to see that it's nearly eleven at night and Dawson has slept the whole way. She wanted to travel as late as we could so he would sleep the whole way and she wasn't fucking wrong which just pisses me off further that she knows him better than I do.

"I'll get him to Facetime you every day while you're away." I don't get the chance to answer, her phone rings, cutting her off. She answers it without hesitation. "Hey." I strain my hearing, I can't hear what is said on the other line but I can tell it's a guys voice. "Yeah, we're not too far now." She pauses as whoever the fuck it is speaks. "He's asleep in the back." That does it, she won't sit in my fucking car and speak to some cocksucker about my son.

"Hang the fucking phone up!" I feel her stare boring into the side of my head. "Now!" I growl.

"Y-yeah, I have to go but I'll see you tomorrow," she rushes to say before ending the call. I cut a glance at her and make sure she can see the disdain in my eyes.

"Who the fuck was that?" Her gaze hardens as she stares over at me.

"Careful, Beck, your jealousy is showing." The low rumble in her tone tells me I've struck a nerve.

"You fucking wish. I don't give a shit whom you let beat that used up pussy." She gasps but I'm not done. "I only give a fuck because if that limp dick, motherfucker is around *my* son, I want to know about it."

"Screw you! I've never done anything to you–" Before she can finish that fucking sentence, I veer off and leave the others to continue on and park on the side of the road. No street lights are visible, so the only lighting is from my headlights.

"Get the fuck out now!" I snap. We both climb out of the car and even though we are both fucking pissed off, we still close our doors quietly so we don't wake Dawson. I storm around to her side of the car, ready to fucking let her have it but the dirty little liar launches herself at me, I catch her without a second thought and hold her against me. The second I realize what I've done I drop her and step back. She stumbles but rights herself quickly.

She smirks up at me and places her hands on her hips with a smug look on her face. "Hm, so you don't like me and my beat up pussy, but you sure as shit didn't hesitate for a split second to catch me."

"Reflexes from playing football," I grit out through clenched teeth.

"I'll pretend that I believe you." My nostrils flare in outrage as I close the space between us. I reach out to grab her and the bitch mocks me by tipping her head and giving me better access to her throat. "Go ahead, choke me, cuss me out, tell me how much you can't stand the sight of me but this time, make sure when you say it your eyes don't betray you." The tremor in her voice alerts me to fact that she isn't as unaffected by me as she wants me to think.

Game on!

CHAPTER TEN

I expect him to wrap his hand around my throat and spew his threats but he doesn't. He cups my face between his large hands and lowers his head until his forehead rests against mine. He drops his mask and allows me to see the lust in his eyes, they burn with desire and my breath hitches at the sight.

His gaze bores into mine as his lips ghost over my own sending a shiver down my spine. "You still know how to get under my skin." He darts his tongue out to moisten his lips and in turn licks my own forcing a gasp from me. He uses that to his advantage as he slants his mouth across mine and kisses me like a starved man. The moment his tongue flicks across mine and the taste of him hits my senses, I moan into his mouth. He shifts his hands, one on the back of my neck and the other on my lower back, as he pulls me flush against him. I wrap my arms around his neck and he thrusts his hips into me. I groan the second I feel how hard he is. I clench my thighs together to try to dull the ache between my legs. He moves his hand from my back to slip in between our bodies and cup my pussy through my leggings.

"Shit," I rasp out at the feeling of having his hand there. He pushes us back until I'm flush against the side of the car.

He shifts his hand and pushes inside my pants. A strangled moan comes from me when he pushes my panties to the side and runs a finger through my slick folds.

"Still so responsive," he says huskily as he buries his face in the crook of my neck and begins to suck. I lull my head to the side to give him better access, moaning as he sucks my flesh into his mouth. He circles my clit with his finger and I'm powerless to stop the sounds from tearing out of me. "Spread your legs, I need better access to this little cunt," he commands and like a junkie begging for her next hit, I do as he says knowing that he is the only who can have me seeing stars. He pushes his finger inside me and I gasp loudly. It's been so long since I've had sex. "Fuck, you're so tight."

I whimper, "Beck, please."

He leans his head back and stares down at me as he lazily pushes in and out of me. "What do you need, baby?" My lids flutter shut at the feelings he is invoking inside me. "Eyes on me always, Valance." I snap them open and hold his gaze as he continues to pump in and out of me.

"I need more," I cry out into the still nighttime air. He uses his thumb to apply pressure to my clit.

"Fuck." I feel my pussy walls tightening on his finger. I'm seconds away from coming on his hand when he yanks his hand free, and I balk at him. His eyes darken as a sinister smirk graces his darkly handsome face. He wipes the finger that was just inside me across my face and forces a shudder to roll through his body.

"Still so fucking easy, Val. Now I know for sure you didn't struggle the past four years." My jaw unhinges as I stare up at him with wide eyes. "I mean, look how easy you gave that pussy up. Bet you sucked dick for a tenner, didn't ya, baby?" Before my brain can register what I'm doing, I lash out and kick him right in the dick. Satisfaction like I've never felt before courses through me when he drops to his knees like a sack of shit, cupping his cock as he roars in pain. I wrench the car door open, grab his phone from the console and drop it on the ground in front of him as he spews out threats.

"Fuck you, Beckett! The only cock that has ever been in my mouth is yours, you fucking asshole!" I shout before I race around to the driver's side. I jam the lock in place and quickly adjust the seat before I pull a U-turn and drive the fuck away. I glance back in the rearview mirror once to see him standing in the middle of the road looking like something out of a horror movie. "What the fuck did you do, Valance?" I whisper to myself.

The whole ride back to my flat, I spend berating myself for kicking him in the dick and stealing his car. I mean, I wasn't a total bitch, I did make sure he had his phone so he could call his friends or an Uber. The moment I pull up outside my run-down apartment, it's close to one in the morning and guilt is gnawing at me for leaving him back there. I know he deserves a dose of humility but he wasn't wrong. I let him into my pants as easily as a hooker lets a guy fuck her face.

Carrying Dawson up to our apartment I freeze at the sight of four flowers and an envelope sitting there. I look around to see the hall is empty but the feeling of being watched doesn't leave me until I step inside my apartment. I place Dawson in his bed before I head back downstairs to grab our bags and make sure that I lock Beckett's car so no one steals it. A car like his in this area is like a beacon.

I snatch the flowers and envelope off the ground as I push the door open and make sure to lock all three locks behind me. I drop the bags in the living room next to the couch—which also doubles as my bed—then head to the tiny kitchen to drop the freaking flowers in the trash. I debate just throwing the envelope out but curiosity gets the better of me and I tear it open, I frown when I pull out a bunch of Polaroid photos, I flip them over and fight back the scream that wants to tear out of me as I drop them to the ground. I cover my mouth with my hand as I stand here with unfiltered fear flowing through me, tears pricking the backs of my eyes. I scream when a loud knock sounds at my door and jump back a few steps. I clamp my mouth closed and stare at the door like it's going burst open any second.

My phone begins to ring in my pocket and I squeal in fright. Another loud bang sounds at the door as I fish my phone out. Tears blur my vision so I don't even see who is calling before I answer and bring it to my ear and don't even get a chance to speak before his shouts come through the speaker.

"I am going to fucking end you, if you fucking–"

"Beckett," I whisper shout as another loud knock sounds out forcing me to back up further away from the door. I can hear the fear in my own voice, he must hear it as well because when he speaks next the anger in his tone is gone.

"What's wrong?" I muffle my sob behind my hand.

"T-that's not you at my door, is it?"

"Where the fuck are you?" he shouts.

"Valance…" I scream into my hand at the sound of my name being called out from the other side of the door. I'm shaking so badly from the fear that I nearly drop the phone. "Baby." I cry into the phone when whoever it is speaks again.

"Answer me!" Beckett's worried shout snaps me out of my stupor.

"Beck, please someone is here and… and I'm scared." When they bang on the door again, I scream. A second later I hear Dawson crying in the room and my fear reaches new heights.

"I'm coming," he growls. "Head to her apartment Corvin, now!" I don't know how he knows where I live but right now I don't give a fuck.

"Momma!" Dawson cries out, and the banging on the

door intensifies at the sound of my son's cry. Call it a mothers instinct or whatever but at the sound of fear in my child's voice everything inside me turns numb. I no longer feel fear for myself or worry about what will happen to me if they manage to get in, my only concern is my son's safety.

"Beckett, whatever happens, you protect our son–"

"Shut the fuck up, Valance!" he roars.

I ignore him as I push on. "You fucking protect him, Beckett, never let him grow up like we did, promise me!" I scream into the phone as I race down the small hallway and close the door ignoring my son's screams. I won't lock myself in there with him in case whoever it is manages to get that door open. I want their focus on me and not my son. "Promise me!" I shout into the phone when he doesn't answer.

"I promise to kill whoever is at your fucking door, I promise to protect our son and I promise to protect you." His words have my knees giving out. I drop to the floor and sob while Dawson pounds on the door behind me, screaming my name, but I block it out. I shut everything out even the sound of Beckett's voice as I fall into a pit of despair. "Valance!" The sound of his booming voice through the phone snaps me out of melancholy.

"Y-yeah," I stutter.

"Open the door."

I frown. "What?"

"Open the fucking door or I'm breaking it down!" I climb to my feet and quickly and open Dawson's door. He leaps into my arms sniffing and clinging to me as he sobs. I stop a couple feet away from the door.

"You're really here? At my door?"

I hear him sigh through the phone. "I'm here, now open the door." I end the call and drop my phone to the floor as I make quick work of undoing the three locks and throwing the door open in time for Beckett to rush forward and grip my face in his hands. His eyes are wild and filled with unbridled rage as he scans my tear-stained face. He looks Dawson over next as Darius and Corvin walk inside my apartment and stand on either side of Beck.

"What happened, Val?" Corvin asks. I nibble on my lip unsure where I even begin but the moment Darius flicks his gaze to the side and I see his eyes narrow in the direction of the tiny kitchen I know he spotted the photos. He bends down and scoops them all up. I bite down on my lip and take a step back. Beck looks from me then to Darius.

Darius turns to me and pins me with a murderous look. "Why the fuck do you have these pictures?" I shake my head, it isn't what he thinks but those pictures paint me in a bad light. Beck and Corvin snatch the photos and both their faces turn pale. "Why the fuck do you have those photos of my girlfriend?" Darius shouts and I flinch.

"I didn't take them," I whisper as I slowly rock side to side trying to soothe Dawson. Beck flicks his eyes to me, gone is the worry I saw moments ago and now a look of untrust is in its place.

"If you didn't take them, then who did?" His voice is devoid of all emotion.

I shake my head again. "I don't know," I whisper.

He throws the photos at me as he shouts. "Don't fucking lie to me!" I whimper as Dawson begins to cry again. Corvin steps in front of the other two, his eyes shining with pity as he stares at me.

"Val, can you tell me how you got these if you weren't the one to take them?" I look down at the photos. There are pictures of Leah and her friends in bathing suits at the beach, the guys lounging out by a pool and each of the photos have in red writing at the bottom.

Who dies first?

"Ever since I moved here, I have been getting flowers, letters, pictures, calls, texts, and emails from someone. I swear Corvin, I never took those photos. I got home tonight and found four of the *Black Mamba*'s by my door and an envelope containing those photos. I… I think I made him mad."

"*Him*?" Beckett grits out, I keep my gaze on Corvin as I answer.

"He… He's sent me photo's before." Corv frowns and shares a look with the other two before focusing back on me and saying.

"Get your things, you're coming back with us."

CHAPTER ELEVEN

Beckett

By the time we pull up to our house, Dawson is fast asleep in the backseat in his chair. Corvin parks his car beside mine as Darius parks his bike on the other side of him. I was lucky when they saw my car veer off earlier as they pulled over a mile down the road. Corvin came and got me while Darius took the others back and met us at Val's apartment when Corv called for backup on our way to her. None of us say a word as we grab her and Dawson's bags while she carries him inside. The moment the door opens, I spot the others sitting in the living room. They all climb to their feet at the sight of us. Leah rushes to Darius and he wraps her in a tight hold. I say nothing and lead the way for Valance to follow me.

I take her to my room on the second floor, drop her bags at the foot of the bed and walk over to pull the covers down so she can put Dawson to bed. After she tucks him in, she brushes his hair from his forehead gently and places a tender kiss on his cheek.

"I love you a million bibby's," she whispers before turning and rummaging through one of her bags. She grabs two walkie-talkie things and sets one up on the bedside table and stuffs the other one in her pocket. "They're baby monitors." I nod and lead her out of the room, making sure to close the door quietly before we head back downstairs.

Nathan, Cody and Corvin sit on one couch while, Katie, Saint and Crue sit on the bean bags. Darius and Leah sit on the other couch. Darius lifts Leah onto his lap to make room for us. I drop into the middle seat while Valance awkwardly takes the end seat, keeping her gaze on her lap. I let my gaze trail over her. She stills wears the same leggings and Ugg boots from earlier but she now wears an oversized hoodie that engulfs her frame, her auburn hair tied into a messy bun atop her head, her cheeks stained with her tears. The silence continues to stretch until Leah growls loudly and shifts off Darius's lap and moves so she is perched on my leg that is closest to Valance who snaps her gaze up to Leah in surprise.

"Corv filled us in on what happened," she says as she grabs Val's hands in hers and smiles kindly. "I am so sorry that this has happened to you, Val. You must have been so scared." Valance's bottom lip begins to tremble as her eyes fill with tears. Leah drops her hands and wraps her arms around her in a hug. Valance buries her face against Leah and cries. It's taking everything inside me not to break shit and unleash my anger, I want to find this cunt and kill him.

"She can't go back there," Corvin says, drawing my attention to him. I nod my agreement.

"I..." Valance starts as she and Leah break apart, then takes a deep breath before continuing. "The school won't allow me into a dorm because I have a kid and I... I can't afford to move." I hear the shame that laces each of her words and it fucking pisses me off. She'll never have to worry about money again!

"Fuck the money!" Saint snaps, drawing her gaze to his. His eyes shine with a protectiveness I have only ever seen in his eyes once when Garrett tried to gay shame Crue. "You're the mother to my nephew and that makes you family,

Valance." The authoritative tone of his voice has both Crue and Katie staring at him.

"I… wow… thank you?" she mumbles out.

"Don't thank us, that's what family does," Saint says. Valance snorts and quickly smacks a hand over her mouth as her eyes widen.

"I'm sorry," she says as she drops her hand. "I just, I wouldn't know what a caring family is like." She cuts a glance at me as she continues. "My family liked to leave scars, not help each other." I turn away unable to look at her. The others gasp and frown, some catching onto what she is saying while the others don't grasp it. "My dad liked to beat me, his way of showing love was leaving scars on me." I slam my eyes closed as memories of the scars on her back slam into me —the cunt used to use the buckle end of his belt on her.

"I hope the fucker dies painfully!" Crue snaps.

"I hope he dies slowly!" Darius mutters.

"He died screaming," I add as I feel all of their gazes on me but I don't meet any of theirs as I slowly turn back to look at Valance. Her eyes are vacant as if she is lost in a memory. I hate that I can read her so easily, Leah distracts me from staring at her when she shifts on my lap and smiles lovingly at me. Leah is the only one who sees through the walls I have around me, not even the guys see me the way she does. The girl didn't let me keep her at arm's length after the night we shared together. Sleeping with her brought us closer but on a totally different level than her and Darius.

"Why do I feel like that wasn't a joke?" Crue asks. Leah searches my eyes, and without me having to say a word she sees the answer in my eyes.

"Darius told me you alluded to covering up a… *crime*, but then that means…"

I hold her gaze as I say, "Just speak your mind, babe." I feel Valance staring at us, judging us and how close we are.

"You weren't joking when you said you had covered up a

murder before. You covered up Valance's dad's murder because… you killed him." Sharp intakes of air can be heard from the others, my focus remains on Leah.

"I told you before, babe, I'm not a good guy and I meant it." She purses her lips, grips my face between her hands and stares deep into my eyes.

"Bullshit!" The venom that laces her tone has my eyes widening. "You listen to me, Beckett Dawson. You are one of the best fucking guys that I know and I won't have you thinking otherwise. When everything went to shit with me and Darius, *you* were there for me. I love you, we all love you and we're all here for you, Becky." She shifts her hands and wraps her arms around my neck. I return her embrace and hold her close. This girl brought me out of hiding, she made me feel again and for that, I will forever be grateful to her.

"Well, I've never felt like more of a third wheel in my life." Leah chuckles and reclaims her place on Darius's lap. He wraps his arms around her and holds her close. "The tension between you three…" Nathan begins to fan himself. Grinding my teeth, I shoot him a glare. The fucker has no sense of self-preservation and winks at me. Darius growls low in his chest and shoots Nathan a warning look.

"Can we get back on track here?" Corvin asks with an edge of annoyance in his tone. Cody shifts and places a hand on his thigh to try to calm him. He tenses at her touch but masks it quickly, unlucky for him though because Cody notices and withdraws her hand with a sullen look on her face. "We're way past the point of keeping shit buried." He cringes. "Pun not intended," he rushes to say while shooting Val a remorseful look.

"It's okay," she says quietly from beside me. "Look, I don't know what any of that has to do with what is happening now, and it won't change the past or present. It's just better to leave it there and move on."

I take a deep breath to calm myself, while grinding my

teeth to keep from lashing out at her. She is so easy to forgive and dismiss what Corvin says, which is dumb, but the night I try to protect her, she sides against me and tosses me away. I did what I did that night to protect her. Did I mean to kill him? No. Am I sorry that I did? Fuck no! He was a piece of shit and the thought of that useless cunt being around my son or having anything to do with him–fuck. I turn to Valance with wide eyes, she reels back when she sees the look on my face.

"That night…you were pregnant." It's not a question. She bites her lip and nods. "Motherfucker!" I roar. I jump to my feet and pace the living room trying to gather my thoughts and calm myself.

"What night? What happened?" Saint asks.

"What difference would it have made?" I stop my pacing and turn to face her, the fact she sits there looking at me with loathing in her gaze has an inferno of hate being inside me. "You still would have fucking killed him!" I move toward her and Valance rises to her feet. I don't stop until we are chest to chin. She cranes her neck back to hold my gaze.

"Ask me," I snarl.

"What?" Confusion is clear in her tone.

"Ask me if I regret it." Her eyes narrow to slits.

"What's the fucking point? I can see it in your eyes that you don't. You forget I know you, Beckett, probably better than all of your friends. Question is, do they know the *real* Beckett Dawson or just the version of you that you let them see?" She doesn't see it coming until it's too late, my hand is around her throat and I shove her down onto the couch, getting right in her face. The others crowd around, shouting at me to let her go. Ignoring them, I hold her gaze. I see the challenge in the depths of her blue eyes.

"You don't fucking know me!" I grit out through clenched teeth, the bitch has the audacity to smile.

"Oh, but I do. I mean, look at you now, Beck. You claim to

have murdered my father for laying hands on me and yet, here you are with your hand around my throat threatening me." I recoil as if she burnt me. She shoots me a smug look as I stare down at her perplexed, am I like him?

"I think everyone needs some time to cool off," Corvin interjects. "It's been a fucked-up night. Val and Dawson are safe here so let's just get some sleep and work on a plan first thing tomorrow morning."

Valance stands next to my bed, the tension between the two of us is palpable. Neither of us can look the other in the eye. For years I pined for her, and mourned the loss of what we shared. The memory of her haunted me for months after I fled on that fucking bus. Looking at her now, I feel nothing but a deep hatred. This woman was once my reason for everything, I fucking killed for her!

"I can't stay here." Her softly spoken words have me tensing and shifting my gaze to hers.

"You can and you will." I expect her to argue again, fight me but what I don't expect is for her to cover her face with her hands and burst into tears. I stand here just staring at her as she breaks down, dropping onto the edge of the bed, heaving. I look at Dawson and frown, how he can sleep through the sounds coming out of his mother's mouth is a mystery to me.

"You don't get it!"

"Don't get what, Valance?" She drops her hands and stares up at me, the pained look in her eyes affects me more than I want to admit. I fucking hate that after all this time she can still affect me like this! I shouldn't even be standing in here with her.

"You think you did me a favor! You didn't, you fucking ruined everything, Beckett, and you don't even see that."

"The fuck are you rambling about, woman?" I snap. There was a time when her tears would have brought me to my knees and I would have done anything to keep a smile on her face but now, it just brings warmth to my insides knowing that she is hurting.

"You killed my father, Beckett, and you don't even care!"

Fuck this!

"Go fuck yourself, Valance," I snarl before I turn and storm out of the room. The only reason I don't slam the fucking door is that my son is asleep in there. I come to a stop when I see Corvin leaning against the wall outside of his room with his arms crossed over his chest. I grind my teeth and pray for patience. I don't know what the fuck his obsession with getting involved in my shit with Valance is, but it's starting to grate on my fucking nerves!

"Is it true?" he asks as I lean against the wall opposite him. It's no surprise when Darius's door opens and he walks out to join this little fucking *pow-wow*. I roll my eyes in his direction when he shoots me a smirk, fucker.

"Is what true?" I snap.

He pins me with a hard glare. "Did you really kill her father?"

I school my features and keep my face blank. "And if it is?"

"Beck, none of us are judging you. You know better than anyone that we don't give a fuck about your past, you have been a closed book since the day we met you. All I am asking is, do we need to do any damage control?"

His response shouldn't shock me but it does. Time and again, these guys prove to me that they are loyal as fuck and I am fucking grateful that I can call them my brothers.

"No. I made sure that there is no way to trace anything back to me or *her*."

"You were just a kid, are you sure?" I look at Darius and pin him with a dry stare.

"Yeah, I am fucking sure. No cops have come knocking, have they?"

"Yeah, I guess you have a point there," D acknowledges. We all stand here in silence for a while. I know that with Valance being here and my past coming back to bite me in the ass I'm gonna have no choice but to tell them everything. "So, does that mean you're not going to Alaska next week?"

I sigh and run a hand through my hair, I have been thinking about that since the moment I found out about Dawson. Truth is, I don't give a shit about leaving Valance behind and going ahead with our plans but I can't leave my son. I know all too well what it feels like to be abandoned by your father and I'll never do that to my son.

CHAPTER TWELVE

I wake before Dawson the next morning and manage to sneak a quick shower in Beck's ensuite. I'll admit, I gasped at the sight of it. It's one of those open-plan showers with a waterfall showerhead. I've never showered in such an extravagant shower before but I mean, when you're a gazillionaire I guess you can afford luxuries like that. Once Dawson wakes, I make quick work of getting him changed and brushing his teeth. He is excited as heck to see everyone, this poor kid has been through so much in the past twenty-four hours and guilt is beginning to eat at me.

"Momma, we go?" I smile down at my little guy and nod. If it were up to me, I would spend the day hiding out in this room and avoiding everyone and everything. I guess the plus side is, I know when I open this door that there won't be a flower waiting for me. I grip Dawson's hand in mine and lead him from the room. The moment I open the door and squeal in surprise when Beck drops backward and stares up at me from the ground. "Becky!" Dawson shouts excitedly. He flicks his gaze from me to smile up at our son before pushing up from the floor and stretching. The moment his shirt rides up, my eyes zero in on the exposed skin, his jeans ride low enough that I'm able to see the bottom of his abs and that fucking *V*.

He clears his throat drawing my attention back to him. I can feel the blush coating my cheeks and push my tongue into my cheek. "Breakfast will be ready soon." His voice is raspy from sleep, and that's when I notice he's still in the same clothes from yesterday.

"Did you sleep out there?" He scowls down at me and doesn't answer, just tuns and leads the way. Dawson practically yanks me after Beck. I wish I shared his excitement. The moment we enter the kitchen, everyone looks at us and the conversation stops.

Awkward.

Dawson pulls his hand free and races over to Corvin, who is at the counter pouring some cereal into a bowl. It warms my heart when Corvin smiles and picks my son up without any hesitation. This is all new to both Dawson and me. All he has ever had is me and I guess you could count Jeff but no one else. A pang of sadness hits me right in the chest. My own mother left me behind as she fled. Whenever I look at my son and think of how my mother just left me, I always get angry. I could never leave my son, ever. My father may have been a piece of shit but kids are programmed to love their parents no matter what. Even when my father beat me, I still loved him.

"Val!" I shake my head and shoot Saint a smile.

"Sorry, I was lost in thought," I mumble.

"All good, want something to eat, Crue cooked?" I frown, not used to anyone cooking for me. When my own mother cooked, it was microwave meals or nothing. I had to learn how to cook via YouTube videos.

"Uh, no that's okay. I think we have imposed enough on you guys—"

"Eat the fucking food, Valance," Beckett growls from beside me. Rather than arguing in front of everyone, I swallow my pride and smile my thanks as I take the plate full of food from him. When I spot the Turkey bacon it takes everything inside me not to moan. I place my plate on the table and turn back to grab Dawson, but Beck blocks my path. "Eat."

Glaring up at him I say, "I need to feed him."

"We got it, now eat. I won't say it again." We stand here in a stare-off for a few seconds but the moment he inches forward, I break it and quickly claim my seat next to Cody. Katie, and Leah sit on the opposite side, and each of them smiles. I try to return it but fail from the look of hurt that crosses Leah's face. I take a deep breath and decide to try to mend the strain between us.

"Leah?" She slowly lifts her gaze to mine, and with the most epic timing, Crue, Saint, Darius, Nathan and Corvin all claim the vacant seats around the table. Beckett is the last to claim the empty seat on my other side. I look over to watch as he maneuvers Dawson on his lap so he can dig into the stack of pancakes Corvin places in front of them. It's such a normal thing to see for most people but the sight of my son sitting on his father's lap has a lump forming in my throat.

"Val?" I look back to Leah and cringe.

"Sorry, I got… distracted." She smiles knowingly, before she can comment on what distracted me I push on. "I owe you an apology—"

"No, no, you really—"

I raise my hand, cutting her off. She clamps her mouth closed and drops her gaze to the table. Darius growls and shoots me a warning look but I refuse to cower. "Leah." I wait for her to look at me before continuing. "I treated you unfairly. I expected you to… help me when I shouldn't have. I am sorry for trying to put you in a position where you had to make an unfair choice." Her eyes widened in surprise. "That day… was really hard." I close my eyes and take a breath, gathering the strength to explain why I lost it the way I did. "My greatest fear is losing… my son. That day I thought my fear was coming true. I had no right to project my anger onto you and I hope you will be able to forgive me."

Her eyes well with tears as a grateful smile spreads across her face. "Of course I can. I'm so sorry for any part I played in that, Val. You have to know there is no way we would have ever let Dawson be taken from you."

Taking a deep breath, I share a secret I have never told anyone. "I appreciate that, but nearly losing him before—"

"The fuck do you mean you nearly lost him?" Beck shouts from beside me and I flinch at the harsh tone of his voice. I swivel around to face him. Dawson doesn't seem to notice the tension between me and his father, which I am grateful for.

"Beckett, I was sixteen when he was born. I had no job, no home, nowhere to go and I sure as hell didn't have any money to care for a child." The growls and sharp intake of air from around the table has shame coloring my cheeks, but I push on. "I was living out of a shelter. I had to rely on donations and the help of others to help me until… Until I met Katelyn."

"Who the hell is that?" he demands.

"Katelyn is the reason Dawson and I are here right now. When the shelter called child services on me, they threatened to take him from me but Katelyn swooped in and told them that I live with her. She worked at the shelter we were staying at. She gave us a home and helped me get on my feet, get my GED and she was the one who pushed for me to apply to CHU." A frown mars his face. I can see a war of emotions in his eyes. I didn't tell him this for him to pity me, I told him so he could understand how fucking hard things were for me.

"Where is this woman now?" Nathan asks. I turn to him and smile sadly.

"She passed away four days after I moved here, she had been battling breast cancer for years." Tears fill my eyes. "She was the strongest woman I have ever met. I had no idea she was sick when I moved in with her. I didn't even find out until after she passed." I swipe the tears from my face and drop my chin to my chest. Silence encompasses the room and I feel shitty for dampening everyone's mood with my sad story, that was never my intention.

"She sounds like an incredible woman." I dart my gaze to Katie, her own eyes are filled with tears. She raises her glass of juice and says, "To Katelyn." I look around the table at the others as they all raise their glasses and follow after Katie, tears of gratitude trailing down my cheeks.

"You will never worry about money." I turn back to Beckett. He stares down at Dawson's plate like it is the most interesting thing in the world.

"What?" I ask hesitantly.

"You will never have to worry about money, you'll never sleep in another shelter and no one will ever take him from you. I'll make sure you *both* have everything." I shake my head.

"No." He cuts his gaze to mine. "I'm not your charity case, Beckett. If you want to buy things for Dawson, then that's perfectly fine but you don't need to spend money on me." He scoffs acting like what I just said is the most absurd thing he has ever heard.

"Money isn't a factor or worry for me. Take the fucking money, Valance." My nostrils flare as embarrassment and anger churn inside me.

"I don't want your damn money! I got here without you—"

"Look how well that's working out for you!" he screams right in my face, and Dawson begins to cry in fright. I reach for him but Beck bats my hand away. I don't know what the hell comes over me. I'd like to say it's a temporary moment of insanity but I also don't want to lie. The sound of a slap rings out around the room, my mouth drops open as I see the red handprint begin to bloom on Beck's face. His angry eyes bore into mine, I gulp loudly.

"Beck!" Corvin warns, but he's not listening, he's too focused on me.

"Leah, come get Dawson." Beck's tone is calm and that scares the fuck out of me. Leah does as he asks and grabs my wailing son from his father. Dawson cries out for me but I'm too scared to move a muscle, feeling like a gazelle who has caught a hungry lion's attention. "Everyone get the fuck out!" I turn to look at Corvin but Beck strikes out and grips my chin in his punishing hold before I have a chance. "You don't fucking look to them." I feel the others all staring but no one says a single word as they follow Beck's order. The moment they all clear out, he grips my throat. Using his hold to lift me to my feet, next thing I know we're gliding across the room until my back smacks against the wall.

"Ah," I cry out when my head bounces off the wall. I try to shove him back he captures both wrists in his one, dropping his hold on my neck he lifts my arms above my head and holds them there. Glaring, I lift my knee ready to do damage to his balls but the smooth fucker must anticipate it, and rather than step to the side, he pushes in closer and wedges his own leg between mine and presses it against my pussy. A gasp tears from me as I stare up at him.

"You like throwing hands?" My mouth opens and but no words come out. It's the lustful look in his eyes that has me lost for words. "Hmm, nothing to say?" he whispers as he leans forward and runs his nose along the column of my neck. Shivers overtake my body. The second his tongue darts out and licks a trail up the side of my neck, my breathing hitches and it takes a lot of fucking self-control to keep in the moan that wants to break free. He sucks the lobe of my ear into his mouth and I'm done for. He presses his leg harder against my pussy and fuck, it feels good. "Look at you, ready to give it up just because I touched you in the right spots." His words are like a bucket of ice water being tipped on me. He pulls back and ghosts his lips over mine as he stares right into my eyes. "He may look like me but because you are a manipulative bitch, I need to be sure." He seals his lips over mine and I gasp in shock. This kiss is nothing more than to silence me and my cry as he yanks strands of my hair out.

The moment he pushes back and frees me from his hold, I slump forward and glare at him. "What the hell?" I shout at him as he stands there with strands of my hair in his hand. He opens his mouth to answer but then it clicks, and I speak before he can. "I would have given you a sample if you had just asked." His eyes narrow but I'm done. I shoulder-check him on my way past but before I can exit the kitchen, I turn and peer at him over my shoulder to find him already staring at me. "When that test comes back as a match, I'm going to laugh in your face because unlike you, I didn't have free time to go find a cock to fill my hole."

"The fuck are you going on about?" I shake my head in disgust.

"It means the last cock I had inside me was yours!" Try as he might, he can't hide the shock from his face.

CHAPTER THIRTEEN

Beckett

Yesterday fucking sucked!

After getting the hair sample from Valance, the guys reamed me out, telling me I was a fucking prick for doing that shit to her. If roles were reversed and this was happening to them, I would want them to be sure as well. I mean, we did just go public a couple of months ago as the owners of BCD'S, it's not that far of a stretch to assume my ex-girlfriend may have seen that and rocked up here with a kid that isn't mine to make me her cash cow.

Nathan, Cody and Katie ignored me and shot me glares each time I passed them, not like I give a fuck about what they thought. My methods of getting the sample from her may not have been right, but she deserved it after hitting me! I've never been struck by a woman before in my life and the fact that she was the first shouldn't surprise me. Valance has always had a wild side and even as teenager, the girl was fucking wild in bed.

Fuck.

I shouldn't be focusing on the fact that she said she hasn't been with anyone since we last slept together... but that was fucking years ago! The last time we slept together she was sixteen which means, fucking hell, that was four years ago!

"Becky?" Looking over my shoulder I see Leah walking out the backdoor and making her way toward where I'm sitting on one of the loungers. It's fucking cold out but I'd rather be sitting out here than inside with *her*. Leah grips the throw blanket from the back of the other lounger and drops down beside me. I remain silent and wait for her to say whatever it is that she came out here to say. "What's going through that head of yours?"

I keep my gaze focused forward as I answer her. "The result just came in this morning. Dawson is my son."

She snorts, earning a glare from me. "Becky, the boy is your twin except for having his mother's eyes." I lean my head back and close my eyes, letting the morning sun warm me as I try to sift through my thoughts and emotions.

"Why can I talk to you so easily but not… you know what I mean," I ask after a few minutes. Talking to Leah is easy, it takes no effort at all for me to confide in her, but when it comes to talking to Valance or even being in her presence, all I feel is agitation and anger.

"Want me to give it to you straight?" I lull my head to the side and nod. She smiles sadly. "You love her." I tense. "From the tid bits that I've heard, she broke your heart and that shit is hard to get over, trust me." I sigh knowing that her and Darius are the experts on broken hearts.

"Valance and me, we were nothing like you and Darius, we were… fuck, I don't know how to explain it but we were a unit, a force to be reckoned with. Nothing could hurt me. I didn't worry about anything because I had her." Pain radiates throughout my chest, I've never told the guys or anyone about my past. When I met them all in high school, they embraced me with open arms, never pushed for me to talk just let me… be with them.

"I feel like you need to tell us all what happened in order

for everyone to understand what *really* happened to you, Becky." A whoosh of air escapes me and I reluctantly nod. She jumps to her feet and rushes inside to grab the guys no doubt. I've never been good at talking or expressing my feelings. I'm not like Saint and Crue, they can talk shit for days. Corvin is a straight shooter and will tell you how shit is. Fuck, even Darius made his intentions known, but me, I don't say shit. I hate being in the spotlight. I found that shit hard when I joined the team, everyone wanted to know who you were and did anything to talk to you. Saint and Crue love the attention, Corvin fucking laps it up as well but Darius and I, we just loved the game not the fame it brings.

"You good with this?" I look to the side to see Leah standing there with Crue, Saint, Darius and Corvin crowding around her. I meet Corv's gaze and nod once. Darius drops into the lounger Leah just vacated, she sits between his legs and leans back against his chest as he throws the blanket over her. The others grab some chairs from the outdoor table and drag them over to us. The moment they are all settled I feel their gazes on me, waiting expectantly for me to talk.

Fuck, this shit is hard.

"We're on your side, brother." I meet Saint's gaze and nod my thanks.

"Fuck," I grit out as I scrub a hand down my face. "Okay, so you all know I transferred to Western Heights High when I was sixteen?" They all nod, that's all they know about my past. I never told them why I had transferred high schools halfway through the year. "Truth is, I never transferred."

"What?" Crue cuts in and asks.

"I dropped out of my last high school, well, fled is probably a better word." I take a breath and try to center myself, knowing I need to remain calm in order to get all this shit out. It's fucking hard to share parts of myself with anyone. It's not because I don't want to but it's because I'm ashamed of what I have had to do in order to survive and be where I am today.

"Beck, none of us give a shit about your past brother. We know *you* and that's all that matters." Darius's words bring a smile to my face and help ease some of the tension inside me.

"Look, I uh… didn't have a great home life or even have anyone there for me. Shit. I don't even remember what my mom and dad looked like or the sound of their voices. I remember coming home from school one day and they were just… gone." I ignore Leah's sharp intake of breath and the anguished look in her eyes as I push on. "I came home a couple weeks before I turned sixteen to find the house empty, most of our shit gone. I thought we got robbed until I found the note on the counter and a crisp hundred-dollar bill." I rest my arms in top of my thighs and drop my head, I have only told one person this story.

"What the fuck happened to your parents, Beck?" Corvin whispers. I slowly lift my gaze to his and smile sadly.

"They won at bingo. They cashed in on the grand prize and decided that they didn't need to take their kid with them on their trip to Vegas. The note said they would be gone for two weeks and to spend the money wisely until they got back. They never fucking came back."

"Oh my God." Tears cloud Leah's gaze as she looks at me. "Beck, if they never came back, where the hell did you live when you came to town?"

Smiling sadly I tell them the truth. "A month after they left and didn't keep up with the rent, we were evicted. I stayed with Valance most of the time. When I couldn't stay there I… uh, I stayed at the local parks or broke into the school gym when it was cold out."

"Motherfucking, cock sucking cunts!" Saint seethes, he's angry but not at me. "I hope your fucking sperm and egg donor got fucked over!"

My shoulders deflate as I answer him. "I didn't find out until three months after they left that the RV they brought was run off the road by a drunk driver. They hit a tree head-on and both of them died. I had to be smart and make sure no one knew or I ran the risk of being carted off to foster care and that wasn't an option. Even when shit went south with Valance, I ran because I refused to be a ward of the state."

"What happened the night you… left Val behind?" Corv asks hesitantly.

"Firstly, you all need to understand that from the start of our relationship, her father beat her. I don't mean he spanked her for being a brat, I mean this motherfucker *beat* her like she was a man. He locked her out of their house in the cold, fed her from a dog bowl, he was a piece of shit!" The four guys and even Leah look fucking disgusted and angry at the picture I have just painted for them. I tell them about how the last night I saw Val went and I how accidentally killed her father.

"How the fuck did you get rid of a body at sixteen?" The skepticism coming from Saint is warranted.

"The trailer park Valance lived at, they were doing some construction so… I buried his body there knowing that they were going to lay cement on top of that area." I cringe remembering how fucking hard it was to drag his fat ass across the lot. The fear that I felt thinking someone would spot me dragging his corpse was a type of fear I had never felt before. Living where she did though, none of the residents were ever sober or coherent, so I had that in my favor.

"Jesus, Beck," Corv utters as he scrubs a hand down his face. I shrug not sure what the fuck to say.

"Did the cops ever do anything?" Crue asks. I shake my head.

"Nah, I tore up the carpet where his body was, scrubbed the floor, burnt everything and the clothes I was wearing, and even made sure to clean the house and remnants of a struggle before I booked it the fuck out of town and got on the first fucking bus."

"You really weren't kidding when you said that you had

covered up a murder before," Saint breathes out and a humorless laugh escapes me.

"Yeah. I'm sorry. I really didn't think any of this would come back and bite me in the ass. When she told me to fuck off, I left for half an hour tops and when I came back, she was gone with her mom. I did what I had to so I didn't end up locked up." Leah's eyes soften as she looks at me and shakes her head.

"You didn't do all of that for you, Becky." I frown.

"What are you saying, Goldie?" D asks her. She keeps her gaze on me as she answers.

"He cleaned up and got rid of the… evidence for *her*. You had nothing to lose, Becky, but you knew she did." I drop my gaze back to my lap and ignore how her words ring true.

CHAPTER FOURTEEN

I decide to take Dawson for a walk around the block while Beck and the others are outside. Katie, Cody and Nathan are all in the kitchen as I pass by them I wave bye. None of them try to stop me which I am grateful for, I just need to get the hell out of here for an hour or so and just take some time for myself without having to worry about the fact that Beckett is watching my every move, analyzing me and trying to work out what angle I am playing. I have nothing to gain from him, I mean the fact he is filthy rich now makes my timing seem odd to show up suddenly but that's the thing, I had no freaking idea about him being well off.

"Open!" Dawson shouts excitedly from beside me. I look down and smile at my little guy as I open the front door. When I see a frown mar his face, I turn and stare down at the welcome mat in horror, sitting right there is an envelope and another fucking flower! "I get it," Dawson shouts, but before he can touch the fucking thing I snap out of it and quickly snag the flower and manila envelope from the ground, slam the door closed and lock it. "Momma, I go!"

"No!" I shout and cringe. Dawson's bottom lip trembles and guilt eats at me instantly. Before I can apologize he begins to wail, loudly. The back patio door opens and Beck stalks inside with a pissed-off look on his face. He darts his gaze from Dawson to me where it lingers for a moment, whatever he sees on my face has his face morphing to one of concern.

"What happened?" he demands as the guys gather behind him. Leah slips up beside Beck, and when her gaze drops to the flower her eyes widen.

"Oh my God!" she breathes out. I bite my bottom to keep myself from crying. Leah rushes toward me and grips my shoulders as peers at me. "Is that from… him?" she asks low enough for only me to hear. I nod unable to speak past the fear that is gripping me. She nods, releases me, and turns back to the guys. "Corvin, come get Dawson and get him a cookie. Beck, the rest of us need to talk, now!" Leah leads me into the living room while Corvin tends to Dawson. The guys follow after us. Saint, Crue and Darius stand around the edge of the room while Leah sits with me on one of the couches. Beck storms across the room and drops down in front of me, the dark look in his eyes is one I know well.

"Talk to me, Vally." I slam my eyes closed at the use of his old nickname for me. The moment he rests his large hands on the top of my legs, I relax instantly. His touch has always been able to ground me and keep me centered.

"He found us," I whisper. Beck's gaze drops to the flower and the envelope I have clutched against my chest, the strain on his face tells me he is trying his fucking hardest not to let me see his rage.

"Vally?" I lift my gaze to his, the torment in his eyes matches my own. "Baby, can I see it?" he asks in a voice too calm to match the look in his eyes.

I shake my head. "You don't understand," I mutter close to tears.

"Explain it to me, baby." The coaxing way in which he speaks has my anxiety calming and the need to rely on him and share this burden with someone other than keeping it to myself is the reason why I tell him.

"He sees everything, Beck. He knows where I am, what I do, and who I hang out with. He even sent pictures to Jeff and threatened him to stay away from me."

"Jeff, he the dick—" I narrow my eyes. "I mean, the guy who called at the cabin?" I nod. "Well, in that case, I may not hate this—" Leah clearing her throat has Beck clamping his mouth closed and shooting me a forced smile. "Open the letter, Vally. We'll deal with the Jeff thing later." I nod and do as he says. I place the flower beside me and tear it open, two photos drop into my palm, I turn them over and gasp. The first one is of me and Beck on the side of the road with his hand down my pants. The second, it's of Beck, Darius and Corvin outside my apartment door the night they came to get me.

"He was watching you the whole time," Leah breathes out. The guys crowd around us but before they can view the first photo, Beck snatches it from my hand stands and shove it in his back pocket. The three guys chuckle, they clearly know him well enough to know that the picture he is hiding is something intimate.

"You do know all I have to do is promise to withhold orgasms from Leah and she'll tell me what that picture is of, right?" Beckett pins Leah with a look at Darius's words. The poor girl looks torn until Darius leans over the back of the sofa and whispers in her ear. "Goldie, you want to be on edge for weeks?" Her eyes widen for a moment before she shoots Beck an apologetic look.

"Sweetheart, after everything—"

Leah cuts Beck off before he can finish. "Becky, I'm sorry but he's stubborn," she whines before she turns to peer over her shoulder and look up at Darius. Beckett throws his hands in the air. "It's a picture of Beck and Val on the side of the road." Darius frowns so she pushes on. "He has his hand down her pants and Val looks… blissed out?" I bury my face in my hands mortified.

"Why the hell are you hiding?" The utter confusion in Beck's voice is the only reason I drop my hands and look up at him.

"What?" He shakes his head as he looks down at me. Corvin enters the living room with Dawson on his hip and Cody, Katie and Nathan following after him. Beck points to Corvin who freezes on the spot and looks around confused.

"He is literally holding the evidence of us fucking." My mouth drops open, Corvin chokes on air, while the others all laugh and I pray for the sofa to swallow me.

"That is disgusting and makes me want to never touch my nephew again, fuck you very much, dick," Corvin snaps as he places Dawson down on one of the bean bags so he can eat his cookies.

"Did you give him a kiss?" I frown at Beck's question.

Corvin looks from me to Beck. I can see the apprehension in his gaze as he answers. "Uh, yeah?" Beck smirks triumphantly then turns to look at Darius with a shit-eating grin.

"Well, would you look at that, D, both Williams siblings have kissed *my dick*." Darius looks murderous, Corvin splutters and shouts curses at Beckett and tells him he'll never touch Dawson again after that comment. Meanwhile, I sit here and look between Darius, Corvin, Beckett and Leah, who has her horrified gaze pinned on me. I stand from my seat next to her. She follows suit and the bickering around us stops when they feel the tension between Leah and I rising.

"You slept with Beckett?" I ask in an even tone. Beckett curses from beside me but I ignore him as I look at Leah. She flinches. Darius rounds the sofa to stand behind his girl in support, I feel Beck shift closer to me and tense.

"Yes," Leah answers, lifting her chin showing me she refuses to feel guilt for what she did.

I nod. "Explains a lot," I mutter, she frowns.

"The fuck is that supposed to mean—"

Leah cuts Darius off before he can continue to have a go at me. "Valance, I won't say sorry that it happened because I'm not but, I will say sorry if finding this out hurts you."

"Honestly, I'm not mad." Relief shines in her eyes. "I mean, it's not like I have any claim over the guy. He's free to stick his dick in any hole he so well pleases." Darius opens his mouth to tear me a new one but I cut in before he can. "Save it. I won't say I'm sorry for what I said because I'm not. I don't give a shit if you and Leah like to spice shit up and fuck around with Beck, do you boo and all that shit. But, I won't hang around here and allow my son to watch his father do that shit." I don't wait for a response as I cross the room, pluck Dawson from his spot on the bean bag and make my way upstairs to pack our things. I'm so fucking annoyed at myself for being such a fool. Him calling me my old pet name lulled me into a stupid false sense of hope.

God, I should have known they fucked from the moment I saw how close they are. Out of everyone in this fucking house, she is the closest to him. He fucking let her in! I forced my way into his head and heart, he willingly let her in, and that fucking stings!

It can't have been more than ten minutes before a knock sounds at the door, I ignore it not wanting to talk to any of them. I continue to pack all my and Dawson's things as I wait for Jeff to arrive to collect us, I text him asking if we could stay with him for a bit and of course, he is a saint and agreed.

The door opens and I flick my gaze up to see Leah standing there awkwardly. "I'll admit, I expected Katie or even your brother to come in here, not you." She bites her lip and nods as she closes the door behind herself.

She clasps her hands in front of herself as I drop onto the edge of the bed where Dawson is sitting playing with his toys. "They wanted to come up but I told them you and I needed to talk." I scoff and roll my eyes. "You can be mad at me all you want, Val, but you have no idea what led to me and Beck sleeping together—"

"I don't care what got the two of you alone in bed together—"

"We were never alone, Valance. Darius was present with us in the… act." I hate to admit it but I appreciate that she is wording things carefully so Dawson isn't able to understand. "Darius and I went through a lot to get to where we are now, Becky was there for me."

"You don't need to explain this to me!" I grit out.

"Yeah I do, you need to understand that it wasn't the… act that brought Beck and I closer, it was the fact that—" She blows out a frustrated breath and runs a hand through her long blonde hair as she tries to form the right words. "Look, what happened between him and me was a one-time thing. Do I love him? Yes. Would I do anything for him? Hell yes. He is my best friend, Valance. I love Cody and Katie but what Beck and I have, it's something not even Darius can understand. We just understand each other, we have both been through some really hard things, we just… get each other." She looks me right in the eyes as she speaks. "I will *never* give him up willingly but, if me being in his life is going to cause problems for the both of you, then… I'll stay away." The pain in her voice has me feeling like a dick for being such a bitch to her, again.

"Leah, I have no right to speak on his behalf or yours. If he chooses to sleep with fifty women then there isn't a thing I can say or do about it." I can hear the bitterness in my own voice.

"You don't get it."

"Get what?" I near on shout at her, frustrated with this conversation.

"He only wants *you*. All I did was help him realize that, he doesn't want me in that way, Val. I mean he may want me around because we are friends, but he needs you. I have been watching the way he constantly gravitates toward you, he watches you all the time, even when you don't see him. Beckett isn't the type of guy to express with words how he feels but he is the type of guy to show you how he feels."

CHAPTER FIFTEEN

"You just had to say something stupid." I turn and glare at Darius, the fucker has been trying to say something for the past ten minutes since Leah went to speak to Valance. I admit, I said what I said as a joke and a way to fuck with Darius for getting Leah to snitch on me, but I didn't mean for Val to find out the way she did that I fucked Leah.

"Shut up, asshole," Corvin snaps.

"The fuck did I do?" Darius sounds like a wounded bitch. Corv points between Darius and me, pinning us with a glare from his spot on the bean bag Dawson was just sitting on.

"You fuckers should have kept your cocks in your pants and out of my sister is what!" I bite down on my tongue, trying hard to keep from laughing. Darius on the other hand has no self-preservation and laughs. Corv jumps to his feet and launches himself on top of Darius on the couch and begins to punch him. Cody attempts to make her way over but I dart my arm out stopping her.

"They're just fucking around," I tell her. Darius can't stop laughing as Corvin promises to break his dick. I shake my head smiling.

"Crue, my dicks jealous now, come play with it!" I slam

my eyes closed and pray for patience at Saint's outburst. Crue being the prick he is skips around the other couch and flops onto Saint's lap.

"Baby, I can't pull your cock out in front of everyone, Corvin and Darius will feel inferior when they see the size of yours." Saint burst out laughing. Katie, Cody and Nathan all follow suit. Darius and Corvin both stop fighting and pin our two best friends with a look that promises pain.

"Your girl was screaming my name last night, you bitches!" Corvin growls. Darius fist bumps him smugly. Cody groans from beside me, Katie just shakes her head, while Nathan stands there with the biggest grin on his face—the fucker loves it when the guys play rough he reckons it gets him off.

"Well, Katie must have been screaming your name that loud you didn't hear your sister screaming, *his*," Saint volleys back and points at Darius, smirking. Corvin turns a shade of red and looks to D who is holding his hands up in surrender.

"He's full of shit. I've never touched her, we just cuddle and hold hands—"

Darius is cut off. "Babe, you are so full of shit your eyes are brown," Leah says as she comes into the room and stands beside me.

"I fucking hate you!" Corv pouts as he slumps back into the couch, crossing his arms over his chest like a toddler. Ignoring the guys I look down at Leah and quirk a brow.

"She'll be down in a minute. Just give her time to adjust and explain shit to her, Becky," she says low enough for only me to hear.

"I don't owe her shit—" Before I can finish, the doorbell rings. Nathan rushes to answer the door as we all stand here and wait to see who it is. The moment the person comes into view, I frown. A dude with dirty-looking blond hair, muddy brown eyes, and a fucking *mustache* stands there. The dude is dressed like a fucking pansy—white polo shirt, dark blue jeans and leather fucking shoes. I mean, fuck me, the dude even has his sunglasses tucked into the front of his shirt.

"Uh, can I help you?" Nate asks.

"I'm here for Val." I instantly tense and step forward.

"Why the fuck are you looking for her?" I snarl. The dude cuts his gaze at me and a look flashes in his eyes that I'm unable to get a read on before he masks it.

"Because I asked him to come." I spin around to Valance walking down the stairs with Dawson on her hip, his bag strapped to her back. She comes to a stop a couple of feet away from me. "We're heading out for a bit—" Before she can finish speaking, I'm right in front of her crowding her space.

"The fuck you are!" I growl. I see out of the corner of my eye the cunt trying to take a step inside my house. Corvin, Darius, Saint and Crue all leap over the sofas and block the fucker from making it inside.

"You can't stop me, Beckett, we'll be back later." It clicks into place then, the fucking pansy bitch is Jeff. She takes a step away from me, and I leap into action, grip her face and smash my lips to hers. She gasps in shock. I use that to my advantage and push my tongue inside her mouth, making sure she can feel with every stroke that I own her. I only break the kiss because Dawson giggles. I pull back an inch and hold her gaze as I speak low enough for only her to hear.

"He lays a single fucking finger on you or *my* son, he won't make it to sunrise." She nods on autopilot and slowly backs away from me in a trance-like state. I turn and wink at Jeff. He shoots me a scathing look that has a smirk tugging at my lips. I move to stand between my boys and watch as he reaches out for Dawson, but my boy turns away from him and looks at me.

"I stay with Becky!" he shouts. Before either of them can comprehend what to do, I'm beside Valance in a second and plucking Dawson from her hold. She turns to me with her mouth open ready to have a go at me I'm sure, but I beat her to it.

"You and Jeffy-girl have fun," I smugly say to her before looking back at the pansy fucker. "*My* son will be staying here with me!" Jeff's eyes widen at my declaration. I don't stick around to hear her reply as I make my way to the game room to hang out with my kid for the day.

It's after eight and I have bathed, fed and put Dawson to bed and yet Valance still isn't back from her little fucking *play date* with pansy boy. She's text to check in on Dawson a few times. I sent pics each time, knowing that even though she is pissed at me this must have been fucking hard for her to leave him here alone with me. Okay, granted Leah, Cody and Katie tagged along with her so she had assurances that I wouldn't take off with Dawson.

After another hour I snap. I pull out my phone and send her a message.

> Twenty minutes Valance!

Her reply comes almost instantly.

> VALANCE
>
> For what?

> For you to get that ass back here!

> VALANCE
>
> LOL

I grip my phone so fucking tight I fear I may actually crush it.

> Fine. Don't say I didn't warn you, little girl!

VALANCE

I stopped being a little girl the moment your
sperm penetrated my egg, dumbass!

Keep talking like that and it won't be your
egg I'm penetrating tonight...

I watch the three little dots appear and disappear for a solid couple of minutes before they stop completely and vanish. Ten minutes have passed and still, no reply comes, I'm about to text her again when a call from Leah comes through. I answer before it can finish the first ring.

"Sweetheart."

"Becky, you need to get down to the beach, now." I stiffen.

"What happened?" I growl.

"Uh, well... don't get mad okay—"

"What happened?" I snap, I can picture her nibbling on her lip and trying not to close her eyes.

"Jeff may have got us some wine and then we played truth and dare—" I groan as I drop my head back and stare up at the ceiling. "Val drank half the bottle when I told her that you leave for Alaska in two days." I slam my eyes closed. "Becky, I'm sorry I thought you had told her," she whispers.

"I did tell her but then, shit changed when I found out she was being stalked," I answer honestly. "Hang tight, stay together and I'll sort it." I don't wait for a reply as I hang up and dial Corvin's number. He answers on the third ring.

"I'm guessing that was you my sister was on the phone to?" I smirk, the girls thought we let them go off on their own with some fucker we don't know, silly things. The moment they walked out the door, Corvin and Darius were tailing them in Corv's car.

"What gave it away? Was it the way she was smiling and had a look of regret on her face because she didn't choose me?"

"I'm gonna break your fucking jaw, you motherfucker!" Darius shouts. Laughter rumbles out of me, loving how I can rile him up so easily.

"Did you have a reason you called or did you just want to fuck with Darius?" My laughter subsides at Corvin's serious tone.

"Leah wants a ride, says they had too much to drink—"

Before I can finish speaking Darius cuts in. "Got it. Get the girls and bring back your girl's boyfriend so he can hold her tonight while you rub one out in the shower to memories of her." Before I can scream at him the line goes dead. That motherfucker is going to pay for that one.

I'm sitting on the porch steps with the baby monitor sitting beside me as I wait. The moment I see Corvin's car pull into the drive, I climb to my feet and shove the monitor into my back pocket. I stand here and watch as Darius opens his door. I shake my head when Leah steps out followed by Darius. Figures, that fucker would have spun Corvin a story about needing to make sure she was safe, so he would allow his sister to perch on his best friend's lap. Crue and Saint come bustling out of the house and make their way to the car, Corv helps Cody out while Saint reaches in on the other side and lifts Katie into his arms. Valance is the last to step out of the car, the four guys look to me asking silently if they should help her, I shake my head subtly.

By the time she makes it to the bottom of the porch steps everyone is already inside and no doubt fucking, thank fuck I had the forethought to leave the TV on in my room so my son won't have to hear the girls screaming. Val grips the rail and slowly lifts her gaze to mine, I search her gaze for a beat and cock my head to the side.

"Faking it are ya?" I taunt, she shrugs.

"Having an alcoholic as a father taught me how to fake it like a pro," she quips.

"Why?"

"Because I knew your friends would hide away so you could yell at me for being stupid and making dumb choices."

"You did make a fucking stupid choice today, you left—"

"Because I couldn't stand to look at you with her any longer!" she shouts.

"The fuck?"

"Fuck you, Beckett, I fucking hate you!" she screams as she storms up the steps and tries to barge past me but I grip her elbow halting her.

"You don't get to yell at me, then storm the fuck off. You ran away once already, Valance."

"Because you fucking killed my dad!" I grit my teeth and drag her into the house not needing anyone to walk past and hear that shit. I drag her ass into the game room, knowing this is about to get loud and I don't want to do this in my room and wake Dawson. "Get the fuck off me!" The moment I kick the door closed I release her with a hard shove, she stumbles a couple of steps before turning and pinning me with a nasty look.

"Come on then, let's hear it, baby," I taunt.

"I hate you!"

"I hate you too, baby."

"You fucked my life up."

"You fucking ruined mine the moment you ran from it!" The composure I had is gone, I'm in her face now. She tries to back away but the moment she smacks into the wall her face falls because she knows I have her trapped. "You fucking left me!" I roar. She trembles on the spot, tears fill her blue eyes and she gazes up at me. "You. Left. Me." I make sure she can hear the anger in my tone.

"I never left you!" she grits out as she pushes into me. "I came back, I jumped out of that fucking car. I may have been angry at you for what you did to my father, Beckett, but I still fucking loved you and would have chosen you every time."

"Bullshit! You didn't pick me, you picked the easy fucking way." She shoves against my chest but I grip her wrists and pin them above her head as I get in her face.

"I didn't have it easy. While you were fucking your best friend's girlfriend, I was struggling to make ends fucking meet to feed our son." She laughs but there is no humor to it. "As it is, I'm behind in rent, I'm about to be taken to court because I'm that far behind on his childcare payments. But don't worry, *baby*, you just keep shoving your cock in any bitch's hole while I struggle to raise *our* son."

"What's got you angrier, Val? The fact I didn't sink without you or the fact I moved on and fucked other girls?" Tears leak from her eyes as she slackens in my hold, forcing me to wrap an arm around her waist to keep her upright.

She slowly lifts her tear-filled gaze to mine and my chest cracks wide open at the vulnerability I see in her eyes. "You got to move on while I raised a part of you every single day. Some days it hurt to look at my own son because of how much he looks like you. I'm happy that you thrived and made something of yourself, good for you for moving on. I admit, I'm jealous that you have."

I frown. "Why?" She tentatively reaches up and cups my face between her hands and smiles sadly.

"Because there is no moving on from someone like you. One day I may be able to let you go but right now, I can't. I've always loved you, Beckett. I'm so sorry you thought I abandoned you. My mom dragged me by my hair to the car, I tried to fight but I was too weak." I release my hold on her and stumble back shocked at her words.

CHAPTER SIXTEEN

Leaving Beckett standing there was one of the hardest things I have ever done, but I can't force him to believe me. After placing a kiss on my boy's head, I quietly slipped into the bathroom to shower. Standing here under this amazing shower head, I let the water wash away my tears. Earlier tonight, hearing the timeline from Leah about Beck leaving in two days hit home. I feel like I just got him back in my life, even if he is angry and hates me at least I get to see him. Do you know how hard it is to see someone you shared a love so strong and deep with, look at you like you are the bane of their existence?

Pray you don't find out because it fucking hurts. When a sob tears from me, I cover my mouth with my hand to quieten them. When a cold draft hits my back, I spin around and nearly slip on the tiles until his arms snake out to steady me.

"Tell me to go and I'll leave." The vulnerability in his words has me stunned speechless, well that and the feeling of his hands on my naked hips has a shiver racing down my spine. He slowly shifts his hold on me until my back is to him, the sharp intake of air that comes from behind me has me tensing, knowing that he can see the scars my father left on me from his belt buckle. "I'm not fucking sorry for what I did to him," he growls. I drop my chin to my chest and slowly turn back to face him.

"They don't hurt anymore." I slowly allow my gaze to travel up his naked legs. His thighs are thick and strong, and the moment my gaze lands on his *hard* cock, my breath hitches.

Sweet Jesus!

It's almost like along with his body his cock has grown as well. He's always had a thick girth, but the length of his cock is longer than I remember… but it's the piercing on the head of his cock has my eyes widening. My mouth starts to water and I quickly swallow before continuing my ogling. God, his body is a work of art. The moment I meet his gaze a shudder rolls through me. Gone is the anger, a look of pure hunger shines in the depths of his pale green eyes. Before another word can be spoken, he clasps my face between his hands and meshes his mouth to mine. I moan the second the taste of him invades my senses. I reach out and grip his hips, loving the shiver that rolls through him at my touch.

Before I can deepen the kiss he pulls back and stares down at me. "I'm not going to Alaska." My eyes widen in surprise.

"What?" He smirks smugly.

"I spoke to the guys, with everything that has been going on with you and this fucker with the flowers we agreed to put it off for a few months." I don't use words, I jump on him, and he grips the backs of my thighs and lifts me until I lock my legs around his waist. I feel his hard length press against me and groan. He leans in and trails kisses down my neck before he nips at the soft skin drawing a strangled moan from me. "Fuck, I missed this," he growls before he wraps his lips around my nipple, sucking hard. I cry out, only for him to tear his mouth free and pin me with a warning look. "Keep your fucking mouth closed. If Dawson wakes up before I get my dick inside you, your pussy will pay the fucking price." My mouth drops open in shock. Beck has always been a demanding fucker when it concerns sex but now that we're older, the edge of darkness that clings to him, has me obeying his demand.

When he sucks my nipple into his mouth again, I bite down on my lip to keep quiet but fuck it's so hard when he flicks his tongue several times over it. "Fuck, Beck!" I whine as he switches sides and pays my other nipple the same amount of attention. I grind against him, trying to find some type of friction. My clit is aching to be touched, and my pussy keeps clenching on nothing but air. He releases my nipple with a pop before claiming my mouth again, this time he tells me without words through this kiss that he owns me. The longer he kisses me and won't touch me the more I grow frustrated needing him to apply a bit of pressure or fucking something to my pussy, it's been too long since I felt his hands on me.

Breaking the kiss he smirks at me. "What's wrong, baby?" The smug edge to his tone tells me the fucker knows exactly what he is doing to me—well, two can play at this game.

"Either shove your fingers inside my pussy or put me down so I can make myself come." The shocked look on his face has me smirking, until his eyes darken. I expect him to give in to my demand, but what I don't expect is for him to cover my mouth with his, draw his hips back and then slam up inside me. I scream so fucking loud into his mouth. Tears prick my eyes. He pulls back and rests his forehead against mine, our breaths are coming in short rapid pants.

"Don't give me an ultimatum because I'll always get my way." I should be pissed off by his words, but the truth is, I'm not. The fucking way he was able to slip inside me with ease is a clear sign that he made me wetter than fucking Niagara Falls.

"Beck..." I moan as he slowly pulls out of me until the tip

of his head is all that remains, before slamming all the way inside again drawing a cry of pleasure from my lips.

"Shut the fuck up!" he growls, before wrapping an arm around my waist and using his other hand the clamp over my mouth to keep me quiet. He continues to thrust lazily in and out of me while maintaining eye contact. I can't explain but him watching me the whole time, adds a level of kinkiness I never knew I craved during sex until now. "Fuck, baby, tell me who this pussy belongs to."

He moves his hand allowing me to answer as he pushes so deep inside me I groan. "It belongs to me," I taunt. His eyes narrow before he slaps his hand over my mouth again. His thrust becomes deeper, more purposeful to the point I break out in a cold sweat and grind down onto his cock as I try to chase my release. I can feel it right there but it's almost like Beck is making sure that I... my eyes widen. He smirks in answer. I bat his hand away ready to curse him out until he silences me with a kiss that steals my breath.

The moment he ends our kiss he speaks. "It's my fucking pussy, Valance, learn it, love it, and deal with it because you aren't leaving again." He smashes his mouth to mine again and fucks me so hard against the wall that I know my back will be aching for days. I wrap my arms around his neck and dig my nails into his skin. When I feel my impending orgasm slam into me, I scream into his mouth as he keeps fucking me like a savage. I don't even get a chance to come down from my orgasm before he is roaring his release into my mouth and he's coming deep inside me. He buries his face in the crook of my neck as we try to regulate our breathing. He spins us around so his back is to the wall and slips down until he's sitting on the tiled floor with me straddling him and his cock still inside me.

I rest my head against his chest and close my eyes savoring this moment. He absentmindedly runs his fingers through my hair massaging my scalp. "So, if you haven't fucked anyone since we were together—" I tense in his hold. "Who the fuck is that dick from earlier?" I sit back and look down at him.

"You are seriously asking me that while your dick is still inside my pussy?" His eyes narrow as he grips the back of my neck and drags me forward until my forehead rests against his. My eyes shoot wide and I gasp when I feel him getting hard inside me, again.

"Who's pussy?" he growls as he uses his other hand to grip my waist and hold me in place as he thrusts up inside me.

"Shit!" I groan, he feels so fucking deep this way. He switches his hold from my neck to gripping my hair. He yanks on the strands until my neck is craned back and my throat is exposed to him. My body takes on a mind of its own and begins to grind down on him. He growls his approval before he sucks my nipple into his mouth, drawing a sharp cry from me. "Beckett," I moan his name like a fucking prayer.

"You like that?"

"Yes," I breathe out. He smirks as I grind down on his cock, grips my waist and lifts me off him before placing me on the tiled shower floor and standing. His cock slaps angrily against his toned stomach. "What the hell?" I grit out as I stare up at him.

"Until you can admit that *your* pussy belongs to me, I refuse to allow you to ride my cock." My eyes widen in outrage. He smiles triumphantly and tries to step past me but I reach out and grip his cock in my hand, halting his movements. Before he can say anything I rise up on my knees and pump him twice relishing in the hiss that escapes him. "Valance..." he warns. I bat my lashes up at him, holding his gaze as I wrap my lips around his cock and moan at the taste of him. "Oh fuck," he growls, reaches behind himself blindly and turns the shower off before gripping the back of my hair and holding me in place.

"Hmm," I moan when he thrusts his hips and his cock slams into the back of my throat, making me gag. I love how he has always taken what he wants and never asks permission. Beckett is a broody son of a bitch who learned at an early age to never cave to the demands of others and always go after what you want.

"Hollow you cheeks and swirl your tongue——" Before he can finish I suck and lick his cock like I know he likes, silencing him. "Ah, fuck yes, baby, like that." I allow him to fuck my face how he likes until I feel his cock start to swell in my mouth. Before he can come down my throat I pull back and release his dick with a wet pop. The shocked look in his eyes almost makes me laugh out loud as I climb to my feet and pat him on the chest.

"Oh, baby, you forget who taught you how to fuck. You and I both know I play the long game better than you ever have. You know the saying, *treat em' mean, keep em' keen.*" It's true, I wasn't a virgin when I met Beckett. I lost it a few months prior to Brady Bourne from the trailer park across town. But, Beck was a virgin and I was the one who taught him.

CHAPTER SEVENTEEN

Beckett

The dirty little sex demon turns, giving me a clear view of her naked, pert ass as she tries to step out of the shower.

Not today.

I snap out my arm, grip the back of her neck and yank her around to me. I don't give her a chance to say shit before my mouth is on hers. She moans the moment I swipe my tongue over hers. I slide my hands down her body, grip the globes of her ass and squeeze, relishing in the whimper that tears from her throat. I swallow the sound and deepen the kiss as I pick her up and carry her out of the shower. I place her on the edge of the bathroom counter, a hiss escaping her the moment her ass touches the cold marble.

I step back and run the pads of my fingers down her body loving the shivers that travel through her at my touch. I run a single finger through her folds and growl my approval when I push a finger inside her, loving that I can still feel my cum inside her.

"Oh fuck," she rasps out as I push my finger in and out of her. I pull it out and ignore the sounds of protest that comes from her as I bring the digit to her lips.

"Suck it." Her eyes blaze with need as she opens her

mouth, sucks my finger inside and swirls her tongue around it moaning at the taste. "You like tasting my cum?" She nods as she begins to bob her head up and down on the single digit causing my cock to twitch at the memory of her blowing me. I yank it free and push in between her legs forcing her to crane her head back in order to maintain my gaze. "Tell me that pussy is mine and I'll make you come so fucking hard you'll see stars, baby." The moment her pupils dilate and her breathing turns shallow I know I've won.

"It's yours." I line my cock up with her entrance and push inside her an inch.

"Say it again," I demand as I reach out and twirl her nipples between my fingers, her head lulls back against the mirror.

"It's your pussy, now fuck it."

Jesus Christ, I have missed this, with her.

I slant my mouth over hers to mute her cries as I slam inside her, relishing in the way her greedy little cunt strangles my cock. I fuck her at a punishing pace, loving the way she goes from pulling my hair to clawing my back and locking her arms around my neck as her orgasm begins to crest inside her. The moment I feel the walls of her pussy start to clamp down I break the kiss, cover her mouth with my hand and reach between our bodies. I pinch her clit. Her eyes snap wide as she arches forward and screams into my hand coming all over my fucking cock. I don't give her a chance to ride out the aftershocks, I pull out, grip my cock and pump myself until jets of cum spurt all over her.

Fuck.

The sight of her spent and flushed with my cum covering her, has a sick sense of satisfaction flowing through me. I reach out and smear it all over her tits, stomach and swipe my finger through it before pushing that finger inside her. I fucking love the sounds she makes. Valance is just as fucking depraved as I am when it comes to sex, she fucking gets off on shit like this, always has. She reaches down, grips my wrist and pulls my finger free before lifting it to her mouth and sucking it clean while looking me right in the eyes.

This girl is a fucking temptress.

◉

"Momma!" I slowly blink an eye open at the sound of my son's voice. I lift my head and peek over Valance's to see him sitting up on her other side. He frowns when he looks at me then his mother who is currently wrapped around me with her face buried in my chest, sound asleep. "Becky like Momma?" I smirk, nothing gets passed this kid.

"How about, I take you downstairs to make pancakes and we leave your mommy sleep?" Dawson beams at me and nods eagerly. I slip out of the bed and grab a pair of sweats, pull them on and quietly help Dawson from the bed and creep from the room. When we make it downstairs, I find Darius and Corvin both in the kitchen. Corv is sipping a coffee and D is making a protein shake. At the sight of Dawson, they both beam at my kid.

"I make pancake with Becky." Corvin and Darius both clap and smile, the more I hear him call me *Becky* the more pissed I get. He should be calling me dad or daddy not calling me by my fucking name.

By the time Saint and Crue clamber into the kitchen, Dawson and I have already finished the first batch. "Well, look who got lucky last night," Saint teases as he slides on to the stool beside Corv. Crue slips up behind Saint and rests his arms over his shoulders, while I pin them both with a warning look.

"If you didn't want us saying anything, then maybe you should have worn a shirt, duh." I frown at Crue after helping Dawson pour another batch of batter on the skillet.

"What?" The three assholes begin to laugh. Darius comes

up beside me and claps me on the shoulder drawing my attention to him.

"I'm guessing Valance is a scratcher," he says as he wiggles his brows. That's when it hits me, she clawed the shit out of my back last night. The laughter that bubbles out of me is that infectious even Darius joins in.

"Shut your pie holes," I say as I go back to helping my boy finish making the pancakes.

"Has anyone seen my phone charger?" Crue asks.

"Yeah, you left it in my car the other day," Corvin answers. Crue ambles out of the room to go grab his charger as the rest of us discuss the upcoming season. "I'm so ready, man, DCU isn't shit now without their bitch of a captain." At the mention of Gary, Darius grows tense.

"I'm worried about what he's up to, I haven't heard shit from Troy," D grits out.

"I know he has visited your dad a few times, but as for school and what the hell he is doing for cash, I have no idea," I answer.

"I haven't heard shit from my dad either," Saint says solemnly. Corv reaches over and clasps our boy on the shoulder offering his support. Devon is still a thorn in our side we need to take down. With everything that has been happening with Valance, I haven't really thought about any of the business side of things.

"We'll deal with him—" Darius is cut off the moment Crue walks back in carrying another fucking flower and a white folded piece of paper.

"We have a problem." The somber tone of his voice has me stiffening. Darius pushes me out of the way so he can take over helping Dawson finish the last of the pancakes. I hold my hand out for him to pass me the paper. Crue shakes his head earning a glare from me. "I don't think you want to see this."

"Give it to me now, Crue," I demand. Crue cuts a look at

Saint who nods for him to do as I asked. He takes a step forward and places the paper in my hand, I unfold it and read the fucking letter.

You thought you could leave and I wouldn't know?

Have you learned nothing in our time together? You can try to run, try to hide but watching you at the beach the other day I could see the look in your eyes, you miss me. Say the word my love and I will get rid of that handsy self-righteous bastard who claims to be our boy's father.

I'll see you real soon, V.

All my love and more.

I crumple the letter in my hand just as Valance and Leah walk into the kitchen. Val's hair is wild and untamed, her eyes are bright and filled with happiness. She smiles at the others but that smile drops off her face the moment she sees the flower in Crue's hand.

"Where did you get that?" she whispers, I hate the hint of fear I hear in her tone. Crue looks to me and Val follows his gaze, that's when I notice she is wearing my shirt and fuck me if I don't love the sight of that shit. "What's that?" she asks, pointing to the crumbled paper in my hand.

"Nothing," I grit out. She pinches her lips to the side as she closes the space between us and pries the paper from my fist, she unfolds it and reads the letter aloud. Once she is finished, she crumples it again and tosses it in the trash, then turns to me with a look of hopelessness in her blue eyes.

"I'm sorry." My brows pull in, confused at why she is sorry. Leah wraps an arm around Val's shoulders and pulls her into her side.

"You have nothing to be sorry for, none of this is your fault, Val."

Val nods, acknowledging Leah's words but says nothing for a moment as she gets lost in her own thoughts. Darius helps Dawson plate the last of the pancakes before sitting him on the counter in the middle of Corv and Saint so he can eat the fruits of his labor. I fucking love my brothers for how well they have adapted and accepted my son as their own. "Where did you find the flower and note?" Val asks as she looks to Crue.

"Uh, on the windscreen of Beck's car." That surprises the shit out of me. Val nods and slowly lifts her gaze to mine.

"He knows who you are, Beckett, he's been watching me since I arrived at CHU. I'm so sorry I brought this on you guys. If… if you want me to go, I get it."

Fuck that!

I close the space between us, pull her out of Leah's hold and crush her against me. She wraps her arms around me and buries her face in my chest. Leah shoots me a knowing smirk before rounding the counter and going to Darius. I know Valance and I still have a shit load of stuff to work out, we may have fucked but we're both still harboring anger toward each other, which will take a shit load of time to work through.

"You're not going anywhere, nor is Dawson. We'll figure this shit out," I say. She pulls back and stares up at me.

"Beck, me being here is going to put everyone in danger." Her argument is as weak as piss.

"We've all lived together before, we'll make shit work," Saint says. Val turns to him in surprise.

"I have a kid!" I narrow my eyes at her.

"Correction, *we* have a kid," I snap.

"And we don't give a fuck, he's our family," Darius says in a tone that leaves no room for argument.

"Fuck!" Valance's eyes bulge out of her head at Dawson's outburst. Darius flinches and backs away holding his hands up.

"My bad," D mutters as he slips Leah in front of him as a shield, earning an eye roll from the blonde. Val shifts away from me to approach our son who is covered in maple syrup and grinning at her.

"Baby, that word isn't okay for children to say, only adults can use that word."

My boy frowns and looks at me. "Becky say fuck." I splutter, the little turd just singled me out!

Val groans and looks to the ceiling before refocusing on our kid. "Well, he's an adult so he can say what he likes." Dawson shrugs and nods then goes back to eating while Val turns back to me with a look of unease in her eyes. "Can we talk?"

Three words no guy ever wants to hear.

CHAPTER EIGHTEEN

I follow Beck out the back and mimic his move when he drops down into one of the loungers next to the pool. It's new for me to be able to ask someone to watch Dawson so I can have a minute alone. Leah practically leaped at the chance to hang out with Dawson when I asked if she could watch him while I spoke to Beck. I'm starting to learn that he is safe with these people. If Beckett trusts them, then I guess that means I can too, it's just hard when I have had no one to rely on but myself since the moment he was born.

"Just say whatever it is that's on your mind." I take a deep breath and steel my spine as I meet Beck's pale-green eyes. He has his emotions walled off from me and I hate that I can't read him when he does that.

"I don't want you to give up going to Alaska because of me." From the way his brows furrow, I can tell he wasn't expecting me to say that.

"What?"

"You can't change your life and plans because I have some crazy asshole stalking me... I'll figure something out—"

"You're out of your fucking mind!" I recoil at his harsh tone. "If you think I'll leave my fucking kid now that I know he exists, then you are stupider than you look!" I bristle at his underhanded insult.

"Screw you, I was only trying to help—"

"How the fuck were you trying to help by getting me out of Dawson's life?" he yells.

"No, Beckett, I was actually just trying to help!" Knowing this is just going to escalate, I stand prepared to make my way inside until he jumps up and blocks my path.

"Don't fucking walk away."

I throw my hands in the air. "Why the hell not? I won't sit here and have you yell at me because you think you have a right," I shout.

"I do have a fucking right."

"No, you don't!"

"You hid my kid, I have every fucking right!" he roars.

"You killed my father!" I scream back. Beck's eyes widen for a second before he schools his features, his eyes fill with hatred as he peers down at me.

"How long you gonna hold that shit over my head, Valance?" His tone is calm and neutral which worries me more than if he yelled.

"When you admit that you had no fucking right to interfere and decide that it was your call to take away a parent from me."

"I don't even fucking know what that means."

"For someone who owns a multi-billion dollar company you aren't very bright!" I tartly reply.

"Yeah well, what do you expect from someone who didn't have a fucking roof over their head until they made it to college because they were too embarrassed to tell their friends they slept in abandoned houses or under a bridge because their girlfriend kicked their ass to the curb." Guilt washes over me. "Don't look at me with pity, Valance, I don't fucking need it. I made something of myself and I'll never be that poor little punk kid who had nothing. My son will never know the struggles that I faced."

"Yeah, and he'll never know what it's like to have his father murdered in front of his eyes." I grit out through clenched teeth.

"You forget my parents are dead as well, I know what it feels like."

"No, you don't."

"Then explain it to me!" he roars.

"My dad was a piece of shit, I know that, but what you don't get, Beckett, is I don't care that he's gone. Your actions that night had a domino effect. I lost my home as well, and unlike you, I didn't have a chance to run. I had a kid to raise on my own." Tears trail down my cheeks now. "I'm mad at you because you doing what you did meant I lost my home." He scoffs and shakes his head.

"How materialistic of you," he snarks.

"Fuck you! Home wasn't a place for me, you dumbass. My home was *you*! I fucking lost you that night, that's what I'm angry about because you have never once admitted you fucked up and left me behind! You. Fucking. Left. Me." Angry tears cascade down my cheeks. Beckett stands there with his mouth ajar and a shocked look on his face. I shake my head and blow out an exasperated breath.

"Valance…" he whispers my name like it's a prayer, but I can't deal with this shit, I'm too emotional.

"Don't, Beck. Clearly too much shit has happened for us to move on. I'll work out somewhere to stay—"

"You're not leaving!"

"Why not? You have made it crystal clear that you don't want me here, so why the hell would I stay? Us fighting and all the tension between us isn't good for Dawson."

"Because I am telling you to stay, you don't have anywhere to go." I glower up at him.

"My apartment may not be much to you but it's our home—"

"You're not listening, Valance, you don't have an apartment." I gasp and stumble back a step.

"What'd you do, Beckett." He shrugs his shoulders.

"Had removalist go in and pack your shit, handed your keys back to the realtor. Oh, I also paid off all Dawson's childcare fees. He won't be going to that place, we'll all pitch in and work out a roster to watch him while you're at school. I'll order him a bed and have it delivered later this afternoon. All your school shit is paid in full and I also contacted your boss at that shitty diner, you won't be working there anymore. Now, if you're done having a fucking tantrum, I'm freezing and going inside." I stand here stunned fucking speechless as I watch him turn and walk back inside. I cringe when I see the claw marks along his naked back.

One week later

Living with Beckett is intense, for the past week it's been nothing but arguing all day and then each night we put our son to sleep in his *own* bed, that Beckett had delivered, and put in his room, then we fuck the night away and get lost in each other. Every morning, we wake to find a fucking *Black Mamba Petunia* on the porch. Beck and the guys had cameras installed but now, whoever this stalker is has a range of different companies delivering them. Beck has forbidden Dawson and I to leave the house without someone with us since I went to the store the other day alone, and the next morning a package arrived with photos of me and Dawson with a man photoshopped into the pictures with us. It's obvious they used a different picture of a random guy to crop into each of the photos. That scared me, but yesterday when another batch of photos came, those ones had me paralyzed with fear. They were pictures of Beck with holes cut into his face and a letter promising to kill him if I didn't leave and return to my apartment.

"Momma, go school?" I shake my head to chase away those dark thoughts and smile down at my little boy, who sits on the mat with Katie coloring.

"Yeah baby, Momma is going with Aunt Leah, Uncle Nathan and Uncle Saint." The day Beck and I had our big fight out back, he told Dawson that everyone in this house is family so he should address them by aunt and uncle, my little guy was thrilled. Corvin, Crue, Darius and Beck amble into the room from working out in the basement. Beck's gaze immediately lands on me and it sends a shiver down my spine. Before I lose the nerve I march over to him and hold out the old leather book I made. He stares at me for a second before looking back at me.

"What's this?" he asks skeptically.

"Back at your cabin, you told me you wanted to know everything, every single detail about our son." I shuffle nervously from foot to foot worried he will hate it.

"Yeah?" I take a deep breath and push on.

"I never knew if I would ever see you again, but in case I did, I wanted you to be able to see all of his firsts, his milestones, and see pictures of him growing over the years. This book is filled with everything. The other day I didn't just go to the store, I went to the storage locker where you had my things taken to get this for you." HIs eyes widen as he looks between me and the book. He tentatively reaches out and grabs it.

"I-I don't know what to say." I smile and lean up on my tip toes placing a quick kiss to his lips before backing away, smiling like a dork.

"Don't say anything, just enjoy learning about your son. There's also a USB in there, I filmed his birth so don't watch that with the guys!" I warn him. Everyone laughs at that. Beck's gaze meets mine and for the first time, when he looks at me, there is no hint of anger only... awe and that steals my fucking breath.

"Eww, can we go before he bones you in front of us." I throw my head back and laugh at Saint. I place a quick kiss on Dawson's head as Cody and Katie stand to grab their bags. The three girls and I have class first up, so Saint is coming with us so we aren't on our own.

"Bye Momma, be good. I stay home with uncles and Daddy." Everyone freezes, and no one utters a single word for a solid minute.

"He said *Daddy*!" Beck whispers. Dawson frowns as he looks around the room to find us all staring at him. Beck's laughter is what breaks the tension, I stare at him in surprise as he places the book on the small table next to the sofa then reaches down to lift our son up and places him on his naked shoulders. Oh God, the sight of Beckett in nothing but a pair of black shorts and our son on his shoulders has me getting hot and breathless.

"Oh snap, Becky is a DILF!"

"Goldie!" Darius snaps at Leah, who just giggles. I nod my agreement because she is right, Beckett Dawson is a *dad I'd like to fuck.* "I'm standing right fucking here!"

"Language!" Saint and Crue shout in unison, making us all laugh again. Everyone has been trying to not cuss around Dawson. My laughter dies off the moment I look back to Beck. My breath hitches when I see the raw hunger in his gaze as he looks down at me. Even when we have had sex recently he has never looked at me like this. Before I can read too much into it, Leah grips my arm and pulls me after her.

"Hurry up before Darius murders me!" she says on a laugh as we rush out the front door. The girls break out into fits of laughter but I don't join in, my mind is still stuck on the look in Beck's eyes. The memory of it sends a shiver down my spine.

"You have a death wish," Cody jests. Leah rolls her eyes and shrugs.

"Darius knows I love him but Becky is just... my Becky." Jealousy runs through me at Leah calling Beck *hers*. I want to stomp my foot and tell her that he's mine but I can't. Truthfully, I have no idea what the hell we are, it's not like either of us have said anything on the matter.

"Well, at least you know where you stand," Cody says solemnly.

Leah cringes. "Corvin still holding you at arm's length?" she asks. Cody nods her head as she drops her gaze to the ground. Saint reaches out and grabs Katie's bag, yanking her back into his side so I quicken my pace to stand on Cody's other side to give them some semblance of privacy.

"He won't even talk to me!" Cody breathes out.

"Why?" I ask.

"I told him I loved him Christmas Eve and he walked out of the room and refuses to acknowledge that I said it. Every time I bring it up or try to talk to him he just walks away or we fight. Before when we would fight, we would have the best makeup sex but now, it's like he can't even touch me." I cringe feeling horrible for my friend.

"Corv is a dick if he can't see how amazing you are." Cody smiles at Leah, but it doesn't reach her eyes. God, I hope that I don't end up like Cody, pining after Beck and watching him fall for another girl, that would crush me.

CHAPTER NINETEEN

Beckett

Crue, Corvin, Darius and I sit around in the living room with our laptops on our laps trying to work while Dawson plays with his toys on the mat. I keep looking at my screen then to the book Val gave me this morning. I'm dying to open it but I'm terrified if I open it all my anger will come rushing to the surface. We fight every day and fuck the night away, honestly sometimes I think we pick fights just so we can guarantee that we'll fuck each night. Having her and Dawson around has been fucking amazing. Waking up next to her each morning feels so fucking right.

"Just open it!" I snap my gaze to the other sofa to see both Darius and Corvin staring at me expectantly. "Dude, we can hear you thinking about it from over here, just open the bloody book." I scowl at Corvin as I close the lid on my laptop and decide to handle the work shit later. But with me now not going to Alaska, we had to hire someone else to take on the task of learning the ropes of each resort. I take a calming breath to try to steady my nerves as I open the book. The first thing that greets me is a picture of a pregnancy test and an ultrasound that has nine weeks written beneath it. I turn the page and see another set of two, one is of Valance and another one is of me from when I was sixteen, I had no idea she even took this picture, on the other page is a note.

Hello my baby,

That's me, your momma, and that handsome man in the other picture is your daddy. You may never get to hear his voice while you are growing inside me but I promise you that his voice sounds better than mine. I'm sorry he won't be here when you arrive, Momma tried to look for Daddy but I couldn't find him. We won't be able to stay at Tammy's for much longer, I don't know where we'll go but one thing I know for sure is, I'll do whatever I have to make sure you'll be safe.

I flick through the book and read all the other notes she has left and view the pictures of Dawson when he was born, his first tooth, she really did document everything for me in the chance we did see each other again. I grab the USB from the back of the book and plug it into my computer, I shove my air pods in my ears before I press play, and immediately the sound of her anguished cry hits my ears. Val looks so young, the fear in her blue eyes cripples me. I search around her for her mother but see no one but the nurses and doctor, fuck, she gave birth to our son alone.

"Miss Karver, you are dilated and can start pushing," the doctor says from between her legs, Val shakes her head.

"I can't. His father should be here, I can't do this without him." My heart breaks inside my chest, I slam my eyes closed as guilt eats me.

"We can't stop this, you need to push," the doctor says, firmer this time. Tears trek down Val's cheeks as she mumbles,

"I'm so sorry, Beck." Tears prick the backs of my eyes, she's so fucking strong. She did all of this on her own. She birthed our child, fed and clothed him even when she was living at different shelters. She got her GED and managed to snag a scholarship to our college because of how fucking smart she is. She busted her ass working to provide for our child, fuck. I made sure she has an account with enough money to set her up for life, I'll never allow the mother of my child to ever want for anything when I have the money to make sure she doesn't need to. "Oh my God." I look back to the screen and gasp, the doctor holds Dawson out to Val. She grabs him and tucks him against her chest as tears trail down her cheeks.

"Congratulations, you have a healthy baby boy," one of the nurses says. Val thanks them but doesn't take her eyes off our boy. I don't realize I'm crying until my tears land on the keyboard. I let them fall unchecked as I watch the girl who taught me how to love, fall in love with our son.

"Do you have a name for him?" a nurse asks. Val nods and smiles down at our boy.

"Yeah, I'll name him after his daddy, Matthew Karver Dawson," she whispers before the video cuts out. I close my eyes and soak in everything I have just seen and read. I've been a real prick to Val since the moment I saw her at the cabin. She didn't deserve that, fuck. I scrub a hand down my face as I think back to that first day, how I took Dawson from her and had the guys drag her away.

"You good, brother?" I open my eyes and look over at Darius and nod. He and Corvin both have looks of concern on their faces.

"Yeah, brother, I'm better than good," I answer.

Crue snorts from beside me and says, "Not for long." The humor in his tone throws me until he hands me his phone to show me a picture Saint just sent him. It's of that Jeff cunt with his arm around *my* fucking girl's waist.

"Motherfucker!" I snarl.

Dawson gasps and pins me with a dirty look. "Daddy, no say that!" I cringe.

"Sorry, bud. How about we go for a ride with your uncles and go surprise Momma?" Corvin breaks out in a fit of laughter.

"And you all say I'm a prick to Cody." I roll my eyes.

"Dude, you don't even talk to the girl unless it's about getting your D into her V," Crue snarks.

Corvin, Darius, and I all lean against my car while Crue is chasing Dawson around the quad pretending to be a monster. I glare at the fucking doors of the English building willing them to open and reveal my girl, her class finished three minutes ago, Leah and the other girls don't have any classes with Val but I know Nat has economics with her this afternoon. She has a break in the middle of the day which she normally uses to tutor other students but not today. The moment the doors open and students begin to pile out of the building I stand tall with Corv and D flanking me on either side. I spot her the second she steps out, her long auburn hair tied up in a ponytail, the jeans she wears hugging her perfectly, and the plain pink Nike top she wears tight across her tits. Even dressed in nothing but jeans and a shirt, she is still the most beautiful girl I have ever seen.

I grind my teeth when that cunt Jeff wraps his arm around her shoulders and draws her in closer. I push off the car and stalk toward her with my boys following closely. At my approach the other students practically jump out of the way to risk not fucking with us, we still rule this fucking school and Jeff is about to learn that the hard way. She frowns as she watches students leap out of the way. The moment her eyes meet mine, understanding dawns in her gaze. She smiles at the sight of me and stops in her tracks, ignoring whatever the fuck Jeff is saying to her as she keeps her focus on me. The second I'm within reach, I shove Jeff away from my girl, grip the back of her neck, and draw her up onto her tiptoes before I smash my mouth to hers, making sure she and every motherfucker around here watching us know who the fuck Valance Karver belongs to.

She grips the front of my shirt and deepens the kiss. I love how she doesn't give a fuck who is around watching me claim the fuck out of my girl. When I pull back we're both breathless and panting, her eyes full of need. Good. I throw my arm around her shoulders cut a quick look to the cunt face who is glaring at me and smirk.

"Later, Jeremy," I say as I turn us to leave.

"It's Jeff!" he calls out.

"Don't give a fuck," I call back, causing Valance to chuckle. Darius and Corvin both shake their heads at my antics but I don't give a fuck, I just made sure every cunt at CHU knows Valance is taken. If anyone tries anything on my girl, they will have me and the boys to answer to.

"You gave me shit for forcing Leah to stay with us and you go and pull a stunt like that?" I shoot Darius a wink over Val's head.

"Difference is, I'm not sneaking around behind Corvin's back." Corv groans and shakes his head.

"Get out now while you still can, being near these assholes isn't worth the stress." All that comment from Corvin does is get the three of us laughing at him. The moment Val spots Dawson and Crue off to the side, she breaks out of my hold, hands me her bag and races over to our son. A smile spreads across my face when Dawson sees his mom. He screams in delight and rushes to her. "There is no getting out for her, is there? She's stuck with your grumpy ass if that look in your eyes is anything to go off of." I keep my eyes on Val and Dawson as I answer Corv.

"Nah, man. She's been mine since we were sixteen and that shit isn't about to change now."

"That guy gives me the fucking creeps." I frown as I follow Darius's line of sight to see Jeff standing off to the side about a hundred yards away, just watching Valance and Dawson as she tickles him on the grass.

"How good is Katie at finding out shit about people?" I ask the guys.

"No idea, man, you're best asking Saint or Crue that one," Corv answers.

"Any chance you could ask Cody? They don't like it when we ask their girl to do illegal shit." Corvin cringes and shoots me an apologetic look as he reach up and rubs the back of his neck.

"Uh, Cody and me… we're uh, not together anymore." My eyes widen in surprise.

"Since when? She was just at the house this morning," Darius quips. Corv looks anywhere but at us as he answers.

"Since I text her telling her that it was over about an hour ago." I shake my head. Darius groans and throws his head.

"You selfish bastard," D whines.

"What the fuck does my relationship status or lack of, have to do with you?" D pins Corvin with a dirty look as he answers.

"Since that's my girlfriend's best friend, you breaking Cody's heart means that Leah is going to be pissed and withhold—" Corvin smacks a hand over Darius's mouth and scowls at him.

"Swear to fuck if you finish that statement the tooth fairy will be visiting your toothless ass tonight!" Laughter bursts out of me and within a second Darius and I are both hunched over and laughing at Corvin, who mumbles about us being fucking pricks and storms off toward Crue.

CHAPTER TWENTY

The next three days go by without a single flower waiting for me on the doorstep. I stupidly allowed myself to believe that whoever has been tormenting has finally grown tired and moved on. What an idiot I am. Beck, Corvin, Leah, Katie, Darius and I all have classes this morning so Saint, Crue and Cody offered to watch Dawson. Not once has Dawson cried when I've left for school, it's strange considering every time I would leave him at the daycare center he would scream and cry for me. Now though, it's like he can't wait to see the back end of me so he can hang out without me around.

"What's going on?" Leah asks as she points ahead to the gathered crowd in the middle of the quad. I squeeze Beck's hand nervous at the sight of the rapidly growing crowd, Corvin slips up beside Katie protectively while Darius wraps his arm around Leah's shoulders drawing her into his side.

"Why are they all looking at us?" Corvin speaks through his teeth. I look around and notice he is right. The closer we get the more attention we draw, this isn't like the other day though when Beck showed up after class. The intrigue in their eyes and some even openly look fearsome as they stare at us.

"They're not staring at us, they're staring at Valance." My

brows jump to my hairline at Beck's words. I shake my head once until the students in front of us drift apart and that's when I see a massive ass portrait of me with Beck's hand down my pants on the side of the road the night we came back from their cabin. I trip over my own feet at the sight in front of me. Beck manages to keep me from falling face-first into the pavement. The photo is daunting but that isn't what has bile rushing up my throat, it's the portrait beside it. Half the size of the one of Beck and me, this one rests on the bench seat staring at me, taunting me almost. It's a picture of my son, but not just any picture, it's a picture of him in a bubble bath. I'm kneeling down beside the tub with my back to whoever the hell took this picture.

"We need to go, now!" Beck growls. Corvin and Darius rush forward and each of them grabs a picture, Beck drags me back toward the car, and I stumble over my own feet too dazed to register what the hell I just saw and read, on the picture of Dawson and me. Written in red across the bottom *you will both be mine*, A shiver of dread runs down my spine.

When we pull up out front of the house, Beck kills the ignition but neither of us make a move to get out. The others pull in behind us in Corvin's car, even as they all make their way inside with the folded in half portraits. Leah and Katie both look back to our car but I can't muster a smile to try to reassure them that I'm okay, because I'm not. Fear has a choke hold on me, they were in my apartment! Shivers begin to overtake my body, and my breathing begins to grow erratic.

"Shit," he mutters before he's reaching over, unclipping my seatbelt, then lifting me onto his lap so I'm straddling him. Clasping my face between his hands he draws me in close until my forehead rests against his. "Deep breaths, baby." I hold his gaze as I try to do as he says but I can't, no matter how much I try I can't seem to get enough air into my lungs! "Fuck," he growls before he smashes his mouth to mine. The shock of his kiss snaps me out of my panic attack and I manage to drag in enough air to stop myself from feeling like I'm about to pass out. The moment he slides his hands down my body and grips my waist, all thoughts of the photos flees my mind as I grind down against him.

A whimper escapes me when I feel that he's hard for me already. Breaking the kiss I meet his heated stare with one of my own and say, "I need you." He grunts his answer, gathers my dress and lifts it until it's situated around my waist. He growls at the sight of my black stockings. I attempt to lift up and try maneuver myself out of them but Beck just grips the crotch and tears them open. Fuck, that's so hot. He pushes my panties to the side and slips two fingers inside me. "Fuck!" I cry out at the sudden intrusion.

"You're so fucking wet for me already," he grits out, before pulling his fingers free and making quick work of freeing his cock from the confines of his jeans. Pre-cum coats the head of his cock, making my mouth water, wanting to taste him but there is no way I can do that in this position. "Shift up." I do as he says and line his cock up with my entrance. I slowly lower myself on him. The moment he bottoms out inside me we moan, sex with Beck is never *just* sex. I know I don't have any other experience with a sexual partner but I doubt it would feel like this. Each time he's inside me, I feel complete like the missing piece of my soul has finally been put back into place.

Reaching out, I rest my hands on the tops of his shoulders and slowly begin to lift up before slamming back down. "Oh fuck," I cry out. He grips my hips and guides me back up, only to slam me back down but this time, he thrusts up inside me and fuck I almost see stars from how amazing he feels this way. Beck is a controlling bastard in and out of the bedroom. Him allowing me to be on top right now is hard for him, but fuck, it turns me on more than I want to admit seeing this God-like man beneath me. He has never looked hotter than he does right now.

"Ride my fucking cock." I obey his command, the sounds that come from him spur me on to bring him to the highest high he has ever experienced. I need this and so does he. We both need this. "Fuck, Val, you feel so good, baby," he moans out as he pinches my nipples through my dress. I cry out and immediately feel my greedy cunt clamp down on his length. My pace quickens as I feel my orgasm cresting. Beck meets me thrust for thrust and within a minute, my head is thrown back and I scream out my release, coming so fucking hard I nearly black out. "Fuck, baby," he roars as he wraps his arms around my limp body, pulls me close and continues to drive into me chasing his own release. He comes with my name on his lips.

Beck and I walk hand in hand into the house. I avoid eye contact with the others as we pass the living room and head for the stairs so I can get cleaned up. I can already feel Beck's cum leaking out of me and soaking my panties, call me sick and depraved but I love the feeling of his cum inside me. There is one thing I love more than feeling it drip out of me though, and that's tasting it.

"Well, if that's not just-fucked hair, then I don't know what is." I cringe and immediately feel my cheeks flame with shame at Saint's jest. The others laugh at his joke, while I try to hide my face and continue on but Beck pulls me to a stop as he faces his friends.

"Har Har, you are so hilarious, Sainty boy. I mean, I do feel for my girl Katie though." I peek up through my lashes to see Saint frowning at Beck.

"Why the fuck would you feel sorry for my girl?" Saint snaps as I look over to Katie who sits beside Saint in Crue's lap with her cheeks as red as mine.

"Because your cock wasn't enough for her so Crue had to man up and take one for the team and help you out." My mouth drops open in shock at Beck's remark. Everyone erupts into fits of laughter as Beck leads me from the room with their laughter following us.

Beck and I make our way back downstairs to join the others after showering. I admit the shower took longer than expected thanks to my need of having to taste Beck's cock. Beckett isn't a selfish lover and of course had to return the favor by eating me out like I'm his favorite fucking meal, my legs are still trembling from the four orgasms he just gave me from his mouth and cock. We find the others all sitting around the dining table with the pictures lying face down in the middle. I look around the room and spot Dawson sitting on Crue's lap watching something on his phone that has a bright smile on his face. I make my way toward him and ruffle my son's hair. He scowls up at me and shakes his head.

"Not da hair, Momma." My eyes widen in surprise. Saint laughs and shakes his head earning a scowl from me. Saint is pedantic about his hair I have learned and it seems that has rubbed off onto my kid. He raises his hands in the air and shoots me a toothy grin.

"Not my fault the kid values his appearance, you'll be thanking me when he's sixteen and looking sharp instead of reeking of B.O." I scrunch my face in disgust as I drop down into the vacant chair next to Crue. Beck claims the other beside me. I look around the table to see Cody, Katie and Leah all have fearsome looks on their faces—Corvin and Darius mirror Beck's angry look.

"I'm gonna set the little guy up with a movie then I'll be back." I smile my thanks to Crue as he leaves the room to get Dawson sorted, all of these guys and girls have been so fucking amazing. Honestly, it still shocks me how easily they have all adapted to living with a child. The guys put deadbolts on the back doors so Dawson would never be able to get out and fall into the pool, baby latches are all over the cupboards, and there is even a baby gate now that separates the kitchen and dining room so Dawson can't get hurt if someone is cooking. We even have baby gates at the bottom and top of the stairs. These people have no idea that what they have done for my son and will forever have me indebted to them without them ever knowing.

"Okay, we need to do something." I nod my agreement. "Val, do you have any idea or an inkling of who might be doing this?" I meet Corvin's gaze and shake my head.

"I've tried for months to figure out who would do this. I don't know anyone. I literally only had one friend until I met Katie and then in turn all of you," I answer.

"Fucking Jeremy," Beck growls from beside me. I roll my eyes and place my hand on his thigh under the tables.

"Jeff, babe, his name is Jeff." I can hear the laughter in my own voice. Beck pins me with a dark look.

"Don't give a fuck." I roll my lips over my teeth to keep from smiling at him, he's jealous!

"Oh fuck me, this is gold!" Darius shouts before laughing hysterically. Leah groans and throws her head back. Saint can't keep the smile off his face, meanwhile Katie, Cody, me and Corvin all sit here confused.

"Shut the fuck up, dick," Beckett grits out. Darius points at Beck laughing so hard his eyes are filled with tears.

"Payback, fucker," he wheezes out before Darius turns to look at me with a mischievous look in his eyes. "So, Val, how do you feel about Pizza with me and the boys." Saint throws his head back and laughs along with Darius. Leah buries her face in her hands.

"You're a real fucking prick, aren't ya?" Beck snaps, causing both the guys to laugh harder.

"You did something with my sister to make him jealous and now he's paying you out for it, right?" Beck grinds his teeth to the point I fear he may break them as he looks at Corvin and nods. Irrational jealousy surges inside me.

"He invited some bitch over to make Leah jealous, so I took her out to get pizza," Beck grinds out.

"Dude, Darius's face was fucking priceless," Crue says as he enters the room again. Darius's laughter immediately cuts off and he pins Crue with a glare.

"Fuck off, I didn't give a shit—"

"You are so full of shit, we all know you were stewing in your rage the second the four of us left your ass here with Courtney," Saint quips.

"Callie!" Crue corrects.

"Cathy, dumbasses," Darius says smugly.

"Chelsea!" Katie, Cody and Leah all shout in unison, causing the three guys to cringe. I can't help the laughter that bubbles out of me, it takes a couple of seconds before the girls join me.

"None of you know what the poor girl's name is?" I ask the guys the moment my laughter subsides.

"Don't feel sorry for her, she was a right cunt and couldn't take the hint that Darius was never up for grabs. He even told her to fuck off at the Thanksgiving bonfire and she still didn't get the hint," Leah says. D wraps an arm around her and pulls her in closer to him.

"It's only ever been you, Goldie." Darius's words have us four girls swooning and the four guys groaning.

"Let's move the fuck on. I don't relish throwing up in my own mouth again," Corvin snarls.

CHAPTER TWENTY-ONE

Beckett

"Okay, let's start with what we know," I say, drawing everyone's attention to me. "Whoever the fuck is doing this has access to Val's apartment, knows her schedule and is following her every move." I see her begin to tremble out of the corner of my eye. I place my hand on top of hers that rests on my thigh and give it a reassuring squeeze.

"Do you have a list of all the students you tutor?" Leah asks her, and Val nods.

"Yeah, I have a schedule that the guidance office sends me at the start of each semester."

"We need a copy of that from the time you first started tutoring. I've contacted Troy, he's going to get us the info for the P.I he uses." Valance turns to stare up at me.

"You want to hire a private investigator?"

"Do you have a better idea?" I volley back.

"Yeah, I do actually." I frown down at her.

"Which is?" I push.

"For me to walk to school by myself for the rest of the week—"

"Fuck no!" I grit out, cutting her off. Her eyes soften as she gazes up at me.

"Beck, listen to me." Her eyes plead for me to listen to what she has to say but she doesn't get it.

"No, you listen to me, Valance. You want to put yourself in harm's way to catch this cunt, last time you were in harm's way I snapped and I lost you. I won't fucking let that shit happen again when I just got you back." I'm not the type of guy who shares feelings or even shows affection but right now, I don't give a fuck. She needs to know that losing her again isn't an option for me. I lost once already and it nearly fucking killed me. I won't survive losing her again. I only started to smile recently when Leah came back into my life because she reminds me so much of Val. I'm close with Leah, not because I have feelings for her but because she reminded me of the girl I fell in love with years ago. Fuck, there it is, I'm still madly fucking deeply in love with the girl I killed for.

"Beck…" she breathes my name like a prayer as her eyes grow misty. I cup her cheek with my free hand, she nuzzles into my touch.

"Don't do this, I can't lose you again," I whisper my greatest fear aloud. I'd go back to living in abandon houses, under a bridge or in the school gym again if it meant never losing her. Without her in my life I was a shell, I hid in the shadows and never really lived… I just existed. She pushes my hand away, stands and swings her leg over my lap to straddle me, not caring that all our friends are watching us as she claps my face and places a kiss to my lips, before resting her forehead against mine.

"You'll never lose me. I've always been yours since we were sixteen and that will never change, Beckett Dawson. You and I are *End Game* material. Let some bastard come and try take you from me and I'll show them that I can be just as ruthless and cutthroat as you. I'm not going anywhere until you tell me to." Gripping the back of her neck, I pull her until my lips ghost over hers.

"That day will never come. You're my beginning, middle and end, baby," I whisper before meshing my lips to hers and showing her without words that she fucking owns every part of me—mind, body, heart and soul. Valance Karver isn't just my first love or the mother of my child, she is my heartbeat.

"Oh my God, Becky!" I break the kiss as Val buries her face to hide her blush in the crook of my neck, as I peer over at Leah who is wiping tears from her cheeks. "I think I love you more than before."

"Fuck me dead, I'm right fucking here, Leah!" Darius snaps angrily. Leah just waves him off, not caring he's butt hurt. I smirk and shoot my boy a wink. He flips me off and slouches back into his chair huffing.

"Must be nice to have a guy profess his feelings," Cody mumbles, earning a glare from Corvin, which she ignores.

"Don't start your shit, this is about them, not us," Corv says, while pinning Cody with a stern look that she matches with one of her own.

"Oh, I'm so sorry, Corvin. How dare I say anything that you don't want to hear. I mean, silly me for thinking that because Darius can admit to his best friend that he loves his sister, that you might be man enough to tell me how you fucking feel!" She pushes back from the table and stands. Corv follows her lead. "You can fuck me but you can't commit to me? You are fucking pathetic—"

"Fuck off with your shit, Cody!" Corvin yells.

"Corvin!" Leah reprimands her brother but he ignores it.

"You want me to stand here and say three fucking words just to make you feel better?" Tears gather in Cody's eyes but she refuses to let them fall at Corv's harsh tone. Cody doesn't know that he can't commit because Lana fucked him over so badly that he can't trust a female anymore. He loved Lana in his own Corvin type of way but that bitch screwed with his head, making him think her cheating on him was his fault. "I can't give you what you want, Cody. I never lied to you. I told you from the start that this could never be more than a bit of fun. You're the one that went and caught feelings when I fucking told you not to!" I can see it in his face, Corv hates that he's hurting her but he isn't wrong. He told Cody he could never give her what she wanted and she agreed to his terms.

"You're right, how stupid of me to think that because we practically live together, spend every free minute we have together and act like a couple that you would be willing to give us a title." The hurt in her voice has me feeling bad for her.

"They don't have a fucking title!" Corvin shouts while pointing toward Val and me. I glare at the fucker.

"Fuck you, she's my girl and we have a fucking kid. It's pretty obvious we're together!" I snap. Val pulls back from her hiding place and stares down at me with a small smile on her beautiful face.

"We're together, huh?"

"Fuck yeah, we are," I growl possessively.

"What's that?" All our focus shifts to Katie to see her pointing to something. Val shifts off my lap and bends over the table to grab something from the back of one of the pictures. She holds up the tiniest thumb drive I have ever seen as she turns to face me. I reach for it but Katie's words have me pausing. "Give it to me, if it's encrypted and has a reversed IP they could track it and hack into the house security system and watch us from the inside." Val eyes widen as she turns and chucks the drive to Katie. "Crue, can you grab my laptop please." He nods and rushes to do as she asks. Val excuses herself to check on Dawson while we wait for Crue to come back. The tension between Cody and Corvin is fucking thick, but right now I don't give a shit about their relationship. I just care about finding this fucker and teaching him a lesson for fucking with my family.

"Uh, not to state the obvious but we all have practice tonight and Katie baby has dance." I groan, I forgot about that. We can't miss practice or coach will fucking kills us. He was fucking cheering when I told him I would no longer be going to Alaska. If we all go tonight that means it will leave Cody, Leah and Val at home alone with Dawson. "Sorry, but I thought I'd just throw that out there," Saint tacks on.

Crue and Val both enter the room at the same. He hands Katie her laptop as we all huddle around her to peer over her shoulder to watch her screen. She plugs the drive-in and immediately starts typing so fucking fast I begin to think she is typing bullshit just to try look cool... until all these windows begin to pop up over the screen.

"What's happening?" Val asks.

"The drive is bugged, they clearly underestimated who you are friends with if they thought this bullshit wouldn't get detected." Val gasps, even in the midst of a fucked up situation, my girl manages to see the good. She's more shocked that Katie called her a friend. Katie continues to type away for a couple more minutes before she brings up a new window that is filled with pictures. She taps on the first one and it's a picture of Val and Dawson at the park as she pushes him on a swing, the next is of Val buying a coffee from the cart in the quad. The next one has me stiffening, it's of Val and me in the kitchen of *this* house, with my face buried in the crook of her neck. I remember that day, it was the day I got a hair sample from her. Katie clicks to the next one and that one has my rage cresting to new heights. It's a picture of Darius, Saint and me out front as we toss a ball around, except all three of our faces are blacked out and up the top in thick bold letters it says,

HE IS MY SON.

Valance whimpers and covers her mouth as she shakes her head. Katie clicks to the last picture and before I know what the fuck I'm doing I'm reaching over Katie's shoulder and slamming the lid of her computer shut. No one says a fucking word as we all stand here silently, my mind is fucking reeling!

"H-how did they get that picture?" Val chokes out. I turn to my girl and grit my teeth hating the look of fear in her eyes. I close my own eyes and try to calm myself, the last picture was of Valance in the shower at her apartment. That wasn't the worst part, it was the black-gloved hand in the shot with a creamy looking substance covering it, I'll give you one guess what the fucking substance was!

"I'm not being a dick right now, but I think after seeing the cum on the sick fucks hand it's safe to assume that whoever this is, *is* a guy." Crue's right, we need to face the fact that Val is being stalked by some sick fuck.

"I have a feeling that whoever this guy is, that he is pissed off," Cody adds.

"Why?" I ask her. She meets my state with a pitying look.

"From what Val has told us about this sick fuck, he has never done anything this bold or anything past leaving a note and a flower until… she reconnected with you."

"What the fuck does that have to do with anything?" Corvin demands, she rolls her eyes and focuses on him as she answers.

"Him seeing Val with Beckett who is Dawson's father, and anyone with fucking eyes can see those two are in love with each other, would spike his jealousy and force him to up his game or risk losing… Val and Dawson to Beck." I hate to fucking admit it but Cody has a point.

"Val, babe, what did the other letters say, the ones before you saw Beck again?" Saint asks. Val scrunches her face as she tries to think back.

"Not much. He would tell me that I looked beautiful, or that he saw Dawson do something and was proud. He would write poems and things like that but nothing—"

Leah cuts Val off. "Wait, who knows Beck is Dawson's father?"

"Why?" Darius asks.

"If Val had no idea that Becky was even here at CHU, then that means whoever is doing this has to know about Val and Beck's past. I've seen Dawson numerous times on Facetime and never once thought he was Beck's until at the cabin, so whoever this is knows about Beck."

CHAPTER TWENTY-TWO

I can see from the strain on Beck's face as he sits on the sofa with Dawson on his lap that he hates the fact he has to leave us and go to practice. Leah asked if I would feel better going with the guys and watching in the stands but the truth is, I just want to hide in Beck's room where he can't see me. I feel so fucking filthy knowing that this sick pervert has been inside my apartment and seen me naked. Bile rises in my throat and I swallow rapidly to rid myself of throwing up again. After Leah announced earlier that whoever is doing this knows about Beck and my past, I've felt sick to my stomach.

"He'll never allow anyone to hurt you or his son." I peer out the corner of my eye to see Darius standing beside me. I've been standing here, leaning against the entryway of the kitchen watching Beckett and Dawson, loving being able to finally see Dawson with his father. The sight in front of me is one I never thought I would ever get the chance to see. I still pinch myself thinking I'm going to wake up and this will all have been a dream.

"You can't know that for sure," I say quietly.

Darius snorts. "Yeah, I do actually, because I know Beckett." I push off the wall and turn to face him. He keeps his gaze focused ahead as he runs a hand through his hair. "When I fucked up with Leah, he stood up and protected her when Corv and I couldn't. He made sure that she was safe, protected and cared for even if that meant putting my girls ass on a plane and getting her away from *me*." He turns to face me and I fight the gasp from slipping free, the anguished look in his eyes tells me this is hard for him to admit. "None of us knew his story. We trusted him anyway because he showed us all time and again that he would ride for any of us till the fucking bitter end. Beckett doesn't care for a lot of people and he trusts only a handful, if you are lucky enough to be one of those people, he'll do whatever it takes to keep you safe even if it means killing to guarantee that."

I search his gaze trying to detect a hint of humor but I see none. He's dead serious, no pun intended. "He killed my father to keep me safe," I whisper. Darius nods.

"I know. He also helped us cover up the murder of the cunt that beat the shit out of Leah and tried to rape her." My eyes widen in shock. "He's a good fucking guy, Valance, one of the fucking best. Trust in him and I promise you that you and your son will be safe, we'll make sure of that, but Beck more so."

"Why?"

"I've known him for years and never once have I ever seen him hold a girl's hand, hug a chick that wasn't Leah or even openly eye fuck one until you. Beck has always been reserved, quiet, guarded if you will and none of us ever cared about that until recently."

"What do you mean?" I push.

"Now that we have seen the real Beck, we are not prepared to lose him and let him retreat back inside himself. Losing you would do that. *I* won't allow that to happen to my best friend so, whatever we have to do to ensure your and

Dawson's safety, we will do it, even if your moral compass can't stomach the way we will handle the situation."

My heart swells inside my chest at hearing how protective he is over Beck. "He is so lucky to have found all of you. Beck didn't come from a family that cherished him. I see now that he found a family in all of you and I am honored to be able to see that."

"You don't just get to see it, Valance, you are our family now and we protect our own. Even if you and Beck didn't get back together, we would all have made sure you and Dawson never struggled or wanted for anything."

I shake my head. "I don't want any money," I answer sternly.

He places a hand on my shoulder and smiles. "It's because you don't want the money why we would give it. Love him like he deserves, Valance, and I promise you that you and I will never have a problem."

"I'll love him till the day I die," I answer with such conviction that Darius can hear the truth in my words.

"Good, because he is a possessive fuck and come game day in two weeks he'll have you kitted out in his jersey just so every fucker knows you're his girl." I smirk not hating that idea at all.

"So, Leah wears yours to every game?" He cringes and shakes his head.

"Uh, she doesn't come to my games anymore." I sense there is a story there but I don't push. "We'll figure this shit out, Val, you have my word that we'll all do everything we can. Troy has a PI guy on it. Beck gave him your number so if anything new pops up you'll be the one he calls." That surprises me that Beck being the control freak that he is, would allow me to receive the information first before him.

"I can skip if you and Dawson want me to stay?" I wrap my arms around his waist, rest my head against his chest and breathe him in.

"Beck, you have to go and you even said yourself that your coach would be pissed at you." I feel him deflate as he wraps his arms around me and holds me close. I'll never tire of the feeling of being in his arms. He places a kiss on the top of my head and steps back. I smile reassuringly and shoo him out the front door with a smile. I close and lock the door behind him and watch through the window as him, Corvin and Darius climb into his car. Crue, Saint and Katie climb into Saint's Jeep. I wave goodbye as they pull out of the drive and don't turn away until they are out of sight. I sigh and make my way upstairs to check on Dawson who is napping.

I make it halfway up the stairs when a knock sounds at the front door, and I freeze. Cody and Leah come into view at the top of the stairs with worried looks on their faces, I take a deep breath and steel my spine as I make my way to the door with the girls following close behind me. "Who is it?" I call out a few feet away from the door.

"I have a delivery for a…" I wait with bated breath for the guy to continue. "Valance Karver?" I frown and shoot Leah a look.

"Just leave it on the doorstep!" Leah calls out, the moment we hear his footsteps retreating Cody rushes forward and peeks out the window making sure he's gone before opening the door, grabbing the package and then quickly closing and locking it again. She hands me the long rectangle box, which has a red bow on the top with a card. I grab the card with shaky fingers and open it.

He will never love you or our boy as I do.

I drop the card and box and jump back a step, the box opens and the contents spill out. *Black Mamba Petunia* flowers cover the floor. I keep backing away until I hit the back of the sofa unable to take my eyes off the flowers.

"What the fuck," Cody whispers.

"Shit, everyone upstairs now!" The panic in Leah's voice has me obeying without complaint. The three of us rush up the stairs and head for mine and Beck's room, closing and locking the door behind us quietly so we don't wake Dawson. I lead the girls into the bathroom and close the door part way as I look to Leah expectantly.

"Why did we run up here?" I ask.

"Whoever the fuck is doing this clearly saw the guys leave and from all of the photo's I've seen, he can't seem to see us on the second floor so I thought this would be the best option." The fact that statement makes sense worries me more than I thought possible.

"What do we do?" Cody asks with a tremble in her voice, I fucking hate that I have brought this fear into their lives. Leah looks to me.

"Should we call Becky?" I nibble on my bottom lip as I debate her question. I know he'll come straight back if I called but then I don't want to give this asshole the satisfaction of knowing he has me riled up and scared. I open my mouth to answer her question but snap it closed when my phone begins to vibrate in my pocket. I pull it out and answer it when I see it's Jeff.

"Hey," I answer.

"Hey, beautiful, how are you?"

"Uh, yeah good." Then an idea strikes. "What are you doing, right now?"

"Nothing, why's that?"

"Do you want to come hang out?" I sigh in relief when Jeff agrees. I give the address. "See you soon," I say as I hang up and shoot the girls a smile, only for it to drop off my face when I see the stunned looks on their faces. "What?"

"Nope, I'm having no part in that. I'll take my chances with the stalker." I frown at Cody confused as hell.

"Beck is going to lose his shit!" Leah rushes to say.

"Why?" I ask as I look between them both.

"The five of them are alpha males, they do not like any other guy around their girls and you my dear friend just signed your pussy up to be denied orgasms." Leah laughs and is quickly joined by Cody as I stand here slightly worried that Leah may be right. No, Beck will be happy that Jeff is here protecting us until he gets home, right?

The moment Jeff gets here, the girls dashed into the games' room and refused to have any part of the *pussy killing mission* as they put it. We quickly stuffed the flowers back into the box and hid them in the kitchen before I let Jeff in. We've been sitting here in the living room alternating between doing homework and playing with Dawson. I managed to reschedule all my tutor session and push them to next week as Beck doesn't want me tutoring anyone until we find out who is behind the stalking.

"That's my boy." I cringe hearing those words come out of Jeff's mouth. I look down to see him and Dawson building Lego and Dawson has managed to make a castle.

"Momma, look." I smile at my boy and clap my hands.

"You are so clever!" I say as I stand to check on dinner. Cody and Leah took over for me, insisting that I entertain Jeff. What they mean, is they want to stay as far away from Jeff as possible so they don't get in shit. "You sure I can't help?" I ask them. They both shake their heads and shoo me from the kitchen. I check the clock on the wall and my anxiety begins to build knowing Beck and the others will be home any minute. I reclaim my spot on the sofa and go back to trying to finish my English paper when Jeff drops down beside me peering over my shoulder at my screen. I shift away slightly not liking being this close to him, the last thing I want is for Beck to through the door and get the wrong idea.

"Ah, you still haven't finished your paper for Moss?" he asks and I shake my head.

"Nope. Between moving, Dawson and… other things, I've fallen behind a bit," I admit honestly.

"Other things as in work?"

"Uh… No, I don't work at the diner anymore," I answer.

"Since when?" I snap my gaze to him shocked to hear a tinge of anger in his tone.

"A while now, why?"

"Just didn't pick you as the type of girl to let a guy buy you." My mouth drops open in shock that he would say something like that.

"Excuse me?" I bite out.

He shrugs his shoulders like he didn't just insult me. "Just saying, it's not a good look ya know. You just meet the guy, quit your job, skip school and move in with him. I mean, don't you think that's a bit confusing for Dawson?" My anger gets the better of me. I place my laptop on the table and stand glaring down at Jeff.

"You need to leave," I growl. He climbs to his feet looking thoroughly confused.

"Why, what's wrong?"

I scoff as I place my hands on my hips. "You pretty much just called me a whore!"

"What? No, I didn't," he rushes to say before reaching out and gripping my arms. I try to pull free but his grip is ironclad.

"Let me go."

"Val, I didn't mean to upset you. I just want what is best for you and my boy."

"He isn't yours!" I shout, and a look of hurt flashes in his eyes. "He's mine and Beckett's son, Jeff. It isn't confusing for him living here because Beck isn't just some random guy, he's Dawson's father, I've told you that before." An angry look over takes his features.

"Is he hurting you?" I balk at him.

"What the hell? Why would you say that?"

"I know you, Val, and this isn't you. You would never let someone like *him* control you. Just say the word and I'll get you and our boy out of here." I stare at Jeff in a new light, he looks unhinged.

"The only person who is going to be fucking hurt is you if you don't get your fucking hands off *my* girl and get the fuck away from *my* son!" I snap my head toward the entry to see Beck, Corvin, Darius, Saint, Crue and Katie standing there. The five guys have murderous looks on their faces. The moment Beck flicks his eyes to me I stiffen at the angry look he shoots me.

"Daddy!" Dawson shouts happily, ignorant to the tension in the room as he runs to his father. Beck schools his features and smiles at our son as he bends down and scoops him up into his arms. "I miss you." Beck's face softens as he gazes at our boy.

"I missed you too, monster. Let's go get you a snack from the kitchen while mommy takes the trash out before Daddy redecorates the living room in the color red."

CHAPTER TWENTY-THREE

Beckett

I shoot Valance a warning look telling her without words to get that cunt out of my house now as I make my way into the kitchen only to slam to a stop when I see Cody and Leah hiding around the corner listening. I quirk a single brow at them. They both shoot me a toothy grin and rush back to finish cooking dinner.

"Get out Jeff, and don't come back!" I hear Valance snap from the living room. Katie brushes past me and grabs a cookie from the jar on the counter and hands it to Dawson with a wink. I know my brothers stayed exactly where they were to make sure the cunt left.

"Val, please, I didn't—" I close my eyes and pray for calm, I can't allow my son to see me lose my cool and coat our living room in the color of his mom's friend's blood.

"She told you to leave, I suggest you do as she says before you don't walk out of here on your own two legs," Darius says in a cold tone.

"Fine. You chose wrong, Val," the cunt snaps before I hear his footsteps heading toward the front door. Unable to help myself, I peer around the corner to see Corvin and Saint block the front door, Darius and Crue close in behind the cunt blocking him in.

"I'll tell you what she chose, a real fucking man that has the money and the means to end a little bitch like you." I smirk, Corvin's tone is void of any emotion. "You ever show your face around here again or go anywhere near Val or *our* boy, we'll break your fucking face and you'll be eating through a straw." Corv steps aside as Saint pulls the door open, smiles wide and says,

"Thanks for stopping by, now fuck off." Jeff shoots one last look at Valance before storming out of the house. Saint slams the door behind him and locks it.

"Here, give him to me." I turn to see Leah standing there with her arms out for Dawson. "Becky, she had a reason for having him here and you need to hear it without Dawson around." The look in her eyes has me handing my boy over and heading back into the living room. Instead of taking a seat, I lean back against the wall, kicking a leg behind me and crossing my arms over my chest as I glare down at my baby momma.

"I can explain—"

I cut her off. "There better be a fucking epic reason why your little bitch boy was in my fucking house and having his goddamn fucking hands on you!" My tone is calm and quiet, she swallows loudly knowing that the fact I'm not shouting or crowding her space means I'm well passed fucking livid with her. She looks around the room to see the four guys standing there staring directly at her waiting for an explanation. Coming home to find some random fucker in our house with our girls isn't something I ever fucking expected to come home to, and I can see from the looks on their faces they are just as pissed at Valance as I am.

She turns back to me as she explains. "I only invited him over because I didn't want you to miss practice—"

"The fuck are you on about? So, you had this little hang

out session planned before I fucking left?" I yell, she recoils and shakes her head.

"No, not five minutes after you all left a delivery came and it was from *him*. Jeff called and I thought it would be okay for him to hang out until you all got back, but I can see now that was a bad idea," she rushes out.

"A really bad fucking idea, Val," Saint adds for good measure.

"What delivery?" I snap. Val motions for us to follow her into the kitchen. The five of us stop in the entryway and watch as she heads to the pantry. When she turns around, she has a box in her hands. She rushes back to me and hands me the box. I pull the lid off and freeze.

"Motherfucker," Darius grits out from beside me.

"There's a card in there," Val whispers. I rummage through the flowers and pull the card out.

He will never love you or our boy as I do. I read the note aloud for the guys to hear, my gaze slowly travels back to Val who stands there looking guilty as fuck.

"Why didn't you call me?" I growl.

"When the delivery came, Leah rushed us all upstairs and had a point that *he* must be watching us and knew when you all were leaving in order to get that delivered. I didn't want to give him the satisfaction of knowing he riled me up and called you, scared."

"Check the cameras," I order Corvin.

"We already did," Val says, stopping Corvin. "It's a legit delivery company. Either he has perfect timing or he had the delivery scheduled for that time. When Jeff called, I thought it was a perfect plan to have him come hang out."

"Doesn't Jeff just have the world's most convenient timing," I snarl. She flinches but says nothing further.

"We need to rework our schedules and change shit up," Corvin says.

"How? We have practice the same time every day, coach

won't change that shit." Saint's right, we can change our classes and shit but we can't change practice.

"Then they come with us every day," Darius tacks on.

"Can we come in the locker room?" Leah asks from her spot next to the stove. Darius shoots her a scathing look.

"The only cock you need to see is mine!"

"For fuck's sake!" Corvin shouts as he shoves Darius away from him. "When you say that shit I'm forced to face the fact my sister isn't a nun and pledged herself to God." Leah chokes on air as she stares at her brother.

"A nun, really, Corv?" she teases.

"Can we focus?" I cut in and say before they continue to bicker and we get nothing fucking sorted. Val moves forward until there is a sliver of space between us, gazing up at me with an apologetic look in her eyes.

"I didn't mean to piss you off. I was just trying to help." A dark smirk pulls at the corners of my lips and I stare down my nose at her.

"I'll deal with you later." She gulps and nods.

"Told you!" Leah shouts drawing my attention and Val drops her head back groaning.

"Told her what?" I ask curiously. Leah smirks triumphantly.

"That having that dick over was a pussy killing mission, I warned her that you would take it out on her orgasms."

"Fucking hell," Darius grumbles as he scrubs a hand down his face in frustration at his girl.

"What's orgasm, Daddy?" I choke on fucking air, then pin Leah with a scathing look at my son's question.

"My bad," she mutters sheepishly.

I step out of the shower and wrap my towel around my waist as I head into the bedroom. I pause in the bathroom doorway as I watch Valance place Dawson in his bed and tuck him in.

"I love you a million bibby's." She places his bibby above his head then straightens. I remember when I first saw that bibby, I was fucking shocked that he would even want that thing near him but I've come to learn that it's his comfort and as long as that raggedy-ass looking thing gives that to him, I'll never complain. Valance turns around and immediately the loving look on her face vanishes. Her eyes travel up and down my body. She darts her tongue out to moisten her lips and I fight the smirk that wants to break free. When she finally meets my gaze, I pin her with a knowing look. She doesn't give a shit she just got caught checking me out from the hungry look in her eyes.

Because I'm a real prick and still fucking angry at her for inviting that piece of shit over, I grip the knot in the towel and yank it open allowing it to drop the floor. Her eyes zone in on my semi-hard cock. I watch her throat move as she swallows rapidly, trying to contain herself and not close the space between us. Leah wasn't wrong, I plan to take her punishment out on her pussy. Val has tried to get me to speak to her all night and I haven't uttered a single word. The lustful look she shoots me has an idea forming in my mind. I hold her gaze as I reach down and grip my cock in my hand, her eyes blaze and her mouth parts slightly as she watches me. A groan slips free when I pump myself, she cuts her gaze to mine and I see the moment she realizes what I'm about to do.

"Aww, fuck no. You get to be pissed all you want but I am not standing here watching you come." I narrow my eyes, the little minx mimics my move and scowls at me. I expect her to clamp her mouth closed and take her punishment like a champ. I know watching me come will leave her on edge all night and that's what I want, but she throws me a fucking curve ball when she grips the hem of her shirt and yanks it over her head. I keep my face blank as she chucks it to the side, unclasps her bra and lets it drop to the ground in front of her. Her full tits are on display, her nipples pebbled and primed for me to suck them, but I remain strong and stay planted where I am as I continue to pump my cock. Pre-cum coats my head and I use it to smear all over my cock, loving the sound it makes.

"Fuck," I grit out. I picture Valance riding my cock in my mind to try to distract me from the real thing in front of me, but the moment she drops her pants and stands before me in nothing but a red lace thong, all thoughts evaporate inside my mind at the sight of that little red triangle covering her perfect little cunt. The dirty little devil holds my gaze as she cups her tits and moans when she flicks her fingers across her nipples. Gritting my teeth, I do my best to try and ignore her and focus on the feelings thrumming through my body as I pump my cock. But, the moment one of her hands shifts and skates leisurely down her flat her stomach and doesn't stop until she reaches the band of her thong, I grit out, "Don't." Her eyes spark with defiance.

"Stop me," she says in a sultry voice. My cock twitches in my hand at her challenge. She pushes her thong to the side and slides a single finger through her folds. "Oh, fuck." A shudder rolls through her and her eyes flicker closed, only to snap wide the moment she pushes a finger inside her tight wet cunt. "Beckett." My name is like a whispered prayer, making my restraint snap—I'll find another way to punish her.

"Get the fuck on the bed and show me how you fuck yourself." She withdraws her finger and brings it to her lips. My breath stutters as I watch her slip that single digit inside her mouth and suck it clean, moaning at the taste. My mouth waters, wanting to fucking taste her, every ounce of her pleasure belongs to me and I fucking detest the fact she even gets to taste her cunt off herself and not me. She slowly stalks toward the bed and crawls to the middle giving me the perfect view of her ass. Fuck, it takes every ounce of control I have not to reach out and smack it, turning it a perfect shade of red. She grabs the pillows and sets them behind herself, reclines back and bends her legs at the knees, spreading as wide as she can before reaching down and pushing her panties to the side. She shows her perfect pink cunt, that glistens in the soft glow of the bed side lamp. "Show me," I growl.

She obeys me instantly and slips a finger back inside her pussy, and her mouth forms a perfect O. She uses her free hand to tweak her nipple as she pushes in and out of herself, moaning. I grip my cock and pump myself in sync with her movements, her head lulls backward and her legs begin to shake.

She's close.

"Oh fuck, yes," she moans out. Fuck it! I'm across the room and knocking her hand out of the way within a second. I don't fuck around as I bury my face in her cunt and moan at the taste of her. "Fuck!" she cries out the moment my tongue pushes inside her tight, wet hole. I glide lower and flick my tongue over her tight asshole, she jolts and that's when it hits me. I use my finger to circle her clit as I prod my tongue in and out of her ass, the mewls coming from her only serve to spur me on. "I'm gonna come," she grits out and not a moment later she grips a pillow from behind her, buries her face in it and screams out her release.

CHAPTER TWENTY-FOUR

I sink back into the mattress and drop the pillow to my side, utterly spent after the soul-destroying orgasm. Beckett's dark chuckle has me tensing but before I can ask him anything, he has me flipped onto my stomach, pushing my legs apart and slotting in behind me. I smirk into the mattress, I knew I'd win. He reaches forward and grabs the pillows before lifting me slightly and placing them beneath my stomach, causing my ass to sit higher. The moment he grips my ass cheeks and parts them, I tense.

"Aww, baby, you didn't think your punishment was coming on my face, did you?" I turn my head to the side and peer over my shoulder at him. The dark depraved look in his eyes tells me he isn't kidding about this. I'm about to protest until he spits and I feel it run down the crack of my ass, he grips his cock and uses the head of it to coat my tight wall of muscle.

He pushes inside me slightly and I lurch forward. "Beckett—."

"You'll fucking take it, Valance, you're going to let me fuck this ass because you defied me today and you need to be punished for that." I balk at him.

"I didn't defy you. I did what I thought was right—" I yelp when his hand comes down on my ass, cutting my sentence off.

"You thought wrong," he growls as he pushes his cock in further. A cold sweat begins to break out over my skin. I try to relax, knowing the more I fight against it and tense the more it will hurt. I know he is pissed off and angry at me but even in this state, I trust him because I know he would never hurt me. If I were to tell him to stop right now, he would, I have no doubt about that. I bite down on my lip to keep quiet and not whimper as he continues to push inside my ass slowly, it fucking hurts. "Rub your clit, it'll distract you." I do as he says and slowly begin to rub circles around my clit. It takes a minute for my mind to focus on the pleasure building inside me instead of the burning sensation in my ass. Beck's right though, I've started to relax and because of that it no longer hurts when Beck pushes further inside me. The moment he is balls deep inside my ass, we both moan.

He pulls almost all the way out before slowly pushing back inside me. It stings for a moment but the third time he does it, the pain bleeds way to pleasure and I begin to feel a whole new sensation taking over my body. I don't realize I've stopped rubbing my clit until he grips that arm and uses it as leverage to hold me in place as he fucks me. The moment he begins to quicken his pace and slam inside me harder my moans grow in volume and I'm forced to bury my face in the comforter or risk waking Dawson.

"Fuck, you feel so good, baby. Tell me you like my cock in your ass." I must take too long to answer because his free hand comes down on my ass cheek again, drawing a loud muffled cry from me. My pussy clenches on air at the feeling of him spanking me. "Answer me!"

Turning my head to the side I look up at him as I answer. "Yes. I fucking love the feeling of your cock in my ass, so much I can feel myself wanting to come again." His eyes spark with carnal need, almost like I have just given him the greatest challenge he has ever faced. He grits his teeth and slams inside me so fucking hard my legs begin to quake.

"I want you to fucking come. You gonna be my dirty girl and come without touching your greedy little cunt?" His dirty words have me moaning and wanting to obey his every word. The harder he fucks me, the stronger I feel my orgasm growing, the feeling is like nothing I have ever felt before. I know without a shadow of a doubt, that this orgasm is going to tear me in half.

"Yes, now fucking punish me and make me come!" I say in a tone I don't even recognize. I sound like a woman possessed but I just can't find it within myself to give a flying fuck. The only thing I can focus on right now is latching onto my impending orgasm and coming!

"Fuck yes, baby, your ass takes my cock so fucking good." He releases my arm and grips my hips in a punishing hold that I know will leave bruises and fuck, the prospect of seeing his fingers bruised into my skin shouldn't arouse me as much as it does. My body takes on a mind of its own and I begin to push back against him, meeting him thrust for thrust, after the fourth time I bury my face into the comforter and bite down on it, trying to muffle my screams as an orgasm like I have never experienced before rips me in half in the best fucking possible way. He doesn't ease me down from my high, he pulls out of me and shuffles off the bed. "Get on your fucking knees." I drag my limp body off the bed and practically fall to the floor. I'm fucking grateful he isn't making me stand because I don't think my own legs would support me. "Eyes on me baby."

I lift my gaze to his and watch his face contort as he pumps his cock in his hand chasing his release. It only takes five pumps before he's throwing his head back and trying to muffle his release behind closed lips as strings of cum spurt across my face, neck, and tits. I keep my eyes closed so I don't run the risk of him getting cum in my eyes, but snap them open the moment I feel him begin to smear his cum all over me, rubbing it into my skin. He kneels in front of me with a possessive glint in his eye as he looks at his smeared cum that covers me before slowly lifting his dark gaze to meet mine.

"You're mine, Valance. Dawson is mine and I will kill anyone that tries to fucking take either of you from me. You're going to sleep with my cum all over you as a reminder of who you belong to."

"Fine. But it works both ways, you have to admit you belong to me too." My tone leaves no room for argument, he lifts his cum covered hand to my face and cups my cheek as he smiles wide.

"I've been yours since the day I met you and that will never change. I meant what I said all those years ago, Valance." I frown not picking up what he's putting down until he takes pity on me and explains further. "I'll always love only you in this life and every fucking other life, it's always been you for me, baby." My mouth drops open in shock. I watch him climb to his feet and stalk into the bathroom while I remain here on my knees reeling.

Beckett Dawson still loves me!

Tensions are high the next morning, everyone on edge and worried about what we might discover today on campus. I have a free morning period and so does Cody, it has taken me nearly forty minutes to convince Beckett not to skip class and stay home with us. He and Corvin only have a morning class and then have the rest of the day off until practice. Cody and I told them we would meet them in the quad with Dawson so we can get to class and they can take Dawson to the park for a couple of hours.

"No more fucking visitors, I mean it." I fight my smile and

nod. Beck narrows his eyes. "Don't fucking push me, Valance."

"If I break another rule do I get a repeat of last night?" I whisper low enough for only him to hear. His eyes shine with lust and I can already feel myself growing wet just from that one look. He bends down until his lips scrape against the shell of my ear, sending a shiver down my spine.

"I'm rock fucking hard now just thinking about my cum all over you." I gasp at his crude words. "Because you were a good girl and didn't shower this morning like I told you, I'll let you ride my face tonight." I slam my eyes closed and try to keep my breathing even, when all I really want to do is drag him upstairs and sit on his face until I'm screaming his name. He pulls back and places a soft kiss on my cheek before resting his forehead against mine.

"I love you," I blurt out, and a slow seductive smirk graces his handsome face.

"Good, because I fucking love you too, Val." My heart bursts inside my chest and I melt into him meshing my lips to his, showing him without words that he is everything to me. Before the kiss can deepen allowing us to get lost in each other further the sound of someone gagging has us pulling apart, laughing. Beck shoots me a wink before he turns to follow the others out the door. I stand here staring at the closed door for a minute, just smiling like an idiot. I'm fucking crazy about Beckett Dawson and the fact that he is mine and loves me seems so surreal.

"You two are so cute together." I spin around to see Cody leaning on the banister of the stairs smiling at me.

I feel the blush coating my cheeks and grin. "I'm so fucked, aren't I?" Cody giggles and nods her head.

"Yeah, babe. Even if you wanted out, there is no way that man is letting you go. Plus, he is fucking loaded and has enough money to chase you around the world." It still stumps me hearing how well off Beck is, you would never think that the five of them are billionaires. They all still go to school, play football and share a house.

"I don't care about his money," I say with a shrug.

Her eyes soften. "Anyone with eyes can see that, babe, all you want is what money can't buy."

"What?"

"His heart, babe. Money can't buy you Beckett's love." I hear the sadness in her tone and guilt gnaws at me.

"I'm sorry, Cody, I didn't mean to—"

She holds her hand up cutting me off. "It's fine. I'm happy for you, Val. You deserve your happy ending. I guess a part of me is green with envy that I won't ever get that with Corvin." I rush over to her and wrap her in a hug. She sniffles and I feel like a right asshole.

"I'm so sorry. I've been so focused on myself and haven't even thought to check in on you." I lead her into the games room where Dawson is currently watching *Raya and the Last Dragon* on the projector screen. We sit on the couches in the far corner so our conversation won't disrupt Dawson's movie. I sit cross-legged, facing her and clasp her hands in mine. "How are you?"

A whoosh of air escapes her. "Honestly, with everything that has been going on with you it's been good at keeping me distracted from the ache in my chest." Her eyes fill with tears. "I love him," she mumbles as the first tear falls.

"Cody, I am so so so sorry, I wish I could knock some sense into him so he could see how freaking amazing you are." She smiles but it doesn't reach her eyes. "Is there anything I can do to help?"

"Actually, there is something you could do for me."

"Name it."

"My little sister is flying in to see me and check out the campus. She wants to apply here and I promised her a girl's night out."

"I don't know if I should—"

"Please, the guys can come as well if you want, but they have to stay on the other side of the club." The thought of having a night out with Beckett and our friends sounds so appealing.

"I don't have anyone to watch Dawson."

"Leave that to me." I look at her skeptically. "I got you, Val. Please, I need this and you will love my little sister."

"If Beck is okay with it then I'm in," I say excitedly.

Cody squeals. "Perfect, I need you with me because my sister wants to murder Corvin for hurting me, so I need to keep her away from him at all costs—" The sound of glass shattering has us both screaming in fright. I leap off the couch to check on Dawson who is pale and clearly scared.

"Stay with him!" I call out to Cody as I make my back into the kitchen. I made it two steps before something smacks me over the back of the head and everything goes black. My last thought is praying that Cody keeps my son safe.

CHAPTER TWENTY-FIVE

Beckett

Strolling through campus doesn't feel the same anymore, now that I have responsibilities. I'm a dad and need to make sure that I set a good example for my son. I want Dawson to be proud of me. Amassing an empire isn't enough, I want to finish school and show him that you can do both. Guys call out to us, trying to garner a flicker of our attention that they'll never get. Girls throw themselves at us or bat their lashes and push their tits out as the five of us walk past. There is only one of us that is free to mingle and even Corvin doesn't seem interested. We come to a stop the moment Lana-fucking-Samuels blocks our path. I glare down at the manipulative bitch. She's flanked by the bane of Darius's existence, Chelsea and on the other side is Saint's stage-five clinger, Sandra.

"Lana, what an unpleasant surprise," Crue snarls. Lana shoots him a filthy look before turning her attention back to Corvin.

"Hey, Corv," she singsongs.

"What do you want, Lana?" Corvin bites back.

"Rude," Chelsea snickers.

"Don't you have someone else to throw yourself at Courtney?" Darius grits out earning a glare from her.

"It's Chelsea!"

"Don't give a fuck." The five of us say in unison, then break out into a fit of laughter. We attempt to push past the trio but Lana cuts in front of Corvin and holds him in place with a hand to his chest.

"Can we talk?" Darius, Saint, Crue and me all shoot him a look telling him not to fall for her shit again.

"Talk about what, Lana? Why all of a sudden are you pouring it on thick again?" He's right, Lana hasn't pushed getting back together with Corv for a while now, what changed?

"Baby, I miss you—" Lana is cut off before she can finish speaking when Leah cuts in front of her brother, smacking Lana's hand away from him.

"Don't touch my brother and stay the fuck away from him." Leah sounds like a right badass. Katie stands beside her friend, staring the other two bitches down. I cut a look to Darius to see him staring at his girl in wonder.

"Who the hell are you?" Lana screeches.

"I'll be your worst fucking nightmare if you don't stay the hell away from my brother." Leah steps into Lana so they are chest to chest. Chelsea and Sandra step forward causing the four of us to close in on Corv and Leah, these bitches won't get away with touching Leah if they try. I look around and see we have gathered the attention of everyone nearby.

"Your brother is the one who slid into my DM's, boo." Leah laughs at Lana which causes the former to turn beet red in anger.

"Babes, your little minion tried to slide into my man's DM's and look how well that turned out for her. My brother doesn't want anything to do with your dirty ass snatch." I cough to try to mask my laughter.

"Coming from the whore who let the team run a train," Darius growls and attempts to cut in and defend his girl, that shit is still a sore spot for him but Saint holds him back.

"What pisses you off more, Lana, the fact I could run a train on the team or is it that only four of them wanted to fuck you because the others were smart enough to know your nasty ass pussy would give them the clap?" Lana gasps and steps back, shaking her head but Leah isn't done. "The next time you come near my brother, my man or any of *my* guys again, I'll make sure that the results of your STI checkup will be blasted all over social media." Leah grips her brother's arm and drags him past Lana, making sure to shoulder-check Chelsea on her way past.

The moment we round the corner, Darius rips Leah away from Corvin and has her pressed up against the lockers claiming her mouth in a primal kiss of ownership. "Fucking stop that!" Corvin hisses. Darius breaks the kiss and smirks down at Leah before stepping back and allowing her to face her brother. "You really got those results?"

Leah giggles and shakes her head. "Nope."

"How did you know she had the clap then?" Saint asks. She shrugs.

"Wild guess and judging from her reaction, I was bang on the money." We all laugh at that, this girl never stops surprising me. "Corv?"

"What's up?" Leah's eyes soften as she looks at her brother.

"I love you. You can do way better than that scabby ass bitch." Darius snorts at Leah's description of Lana.

"Leah, stop. What happens between me and Cody doesn't concern you—" Corvin is cut off by the sound of his phone ringing, he pulls it out of his pocket and groans. I peer over to see it's Cody calling. He sends the call to voicemail only for it to ring again but this time he lets it ring out. I tune the others out as I pull my phone out of my own pocket and shoot a message to Val, I just want to make sure that Cody wasn't calling because something happened. As the seconds tick by and the three little dots don't appear I decide to send another text.

Baby, you good?

I follow after the others as they continue on but worry is churning inside me, something doesn't feel right. I don't know how to explain it but I have this gut feeling something is wrong. "Corvin?" I call out, everyone halts in the middle of the busy corridor as students continue to brush past us making their way to class.

"What's up?" I know I'm probably overreacting but I need to be sure or I'll never be able to sit through a two-hour lecture on Economics.

"Can I use your phone?" I say as I hold my hand out, he shoots me a quizzical look but never the less, hands me his phone. I unlock and see he has a voicemail from Cody, I ignore it and immediately hit re-dial. My worry amplifies as the phone continues to ring, just as I'm about to hang up Cody finally answers.

"C-Corvin?" My blood turns to ice at the weakened sound of Cody's voice. "H-help…"

"Cody? Cody, what happened?" I shout but the line goes dead, Corvin and the others are on me, shouting at me to answer them but I can't. I turn and run as fucking fast as I can back to my girl and son and pray like fuck that I'm not too late to save them. If that cunt has done anything to hurt either of them, I'll fucking kill the cunt with my bare fucking hands.

My car is sideways as I take the turn onto our street. Corvin grips the *oh shit* handle above his head while the other three guys smack around in the backseat. I yank the wheel and practically drift into the driveway, slam it in park and leap from the car, not even caring that I left it running as I race across the yard, then up the porch steps only to slam to a halt at the sight. The same window by the front door Leah broke a couple of months ago is broken. The front door is wide open, fear grips me as I begin to worry about what I might find inside the house. Corvin shoves past me and races into the house.

"Cody?" he shouts. I snap out of it and follow after him. "Cody?" he calls out again as we all begin to look around. Saint and Crue race up the stairs as Corv, D and me check downstairs, I head for the games room and slam to a stop.

"Corvin!" I shout and dart forward dropping to my knees beside Cody. She lays in a pool of blood with a knife sticking out of her stomach, she's deathly pale.

"Oh, God, no!" Corvin screams as he comes into the room. He pushes me out of the way and drops down beside her, his hands ghost over her body scared to touch her in case he causes more pain. A small whimper escapes Cody and Corv sighs in relief as he drops to his ass and pulls her limp body between his open legs. I look up at my friend to see tears rolling down his cheeks. Darius, Saint and Crue rush into the room and freeze at the sight. I look to them in the hope that they may have found my family. Saint shakes his head telling me they found nothing, call me a cunt but a part of me glad my girl and son aren't laying somewhere around here bleeding out. "Call a fucking ambulance!" Corvin screams as he reaches down and tries to apply pressure to Cody's wound. "I'm here, baby. I got you, you're gonna be just fine."

"C-Corv?" I hear the strain in her voice and my heart sinks. Crue rushes from the room to call 911, while the rest of us sit here helplessly and watch our best friend breakdown in front of us. He may not have said the words aloud but I know Corvin loves Cody. He's just scared to take that leap of faith again after Lana fucked him over.

"I'm here, baby." His tone is thick with emotion, he looks down at her and smiles when her eyes flutter open.

"Val… gone." A pained sound escapes me. Cody's head lulls lazily to the side as she looks at me. The look in her eyes has me choking up, Cody isn't going to make it. "D, closet… I kept safe." I frown not understanding a fucking word she is saying but I nod regardless to appease her and keep her at ease.

"Don't talk, baby, save your strength, okay? You're gonna be fine," Corvin says through his tears. Crue rushes into the room then.

"They're on their way."

"Hear that, baby, help is on the way." Corvin forces calm into his voice as he speaks to Cody and smiles down at her. Her breaths are coming in short gasps, her body limp and pale. I reach out to clasp her hand in mind and I feel how fucking cold she is. Corv darts his gaze to me, I see in his eyes he wants me to tell him she is going to be fine but I can't. "Fuck off, Beckett!" he screams in my face before he gathers her up and holds her across his lap. Blood coats his hands and clothes, he cups her cheek and tilts her face up to his. "Open your eyes, Cody, please don't fucking die, baby." The broken sound of his voice kills me.

"Darius?" The sound of Leah's voice snaps D out of his stupor. Katie and Leah drove back in Saint's jeep. D turns to rush out of the room and keep the girls out, but he's too late. Leah and Katie burst into the room like a storm. "Cody!" Leah screams, but before she can get to Cody, Darius wraps his arms around her and hauls her back. Saint and Crue hold Katie back, both girls crying hysterically for their friend.

"Cody?" Corv whispers brokenly, her eyes flutter open slowly. I can see it's taken great strength for her to just open her eyes. Her breathing sounds like a pack-a-day smoker. A sob rips out of Corvin, and he places a soft kiss to her lips, then rests his forehead against hers. His tears fall onto Cody's pale face. "I love you, Cody, so fucking much so you can't leave me, baby, please." Cody's lip twitches in a small smile. She tries to lift her hand to cup Corv's face, but she's too weak. He grips her hand and holds it against his face for her as I hear sirens in the distance. Good, they're close.

"Love… you," she breathes out, then her whole body goes limp in Corvin's hold.

"Cody?" Corv whispers as he drops her hand and cups her face. Her eyes are open but you can see it in the depths of her green eyes, she's gone. "Cody, wake up!" he screams as he begins to shake her. "Wake up, don't you fucking leave me!" he screams, and Leah and Katie's screams pierce my ears and force me into action. I push forward and lay a hand on Corvin's shoulder, he smacks it away and glares at me through his tears. "Fuck off, she's fine!" A pained sound that has my chest cracking open for my friend tears from his throat.

"She's gone, Corv," I whisper through my own tears.

'No! Fuck, please, God no. Please, please, someone fucking help me!" he screams, holding Cody's lifeless body against him. I fall back onto my ass and watch helplessly as Corvin screams for help and begs God to give her back to him.

CHAPTER TWENTY-SIX

Valance

My head is throbbing. I can't open my eyes. A whimper escapes me before a cloth is placed over my mouth and nose, then everything begins to fade….

I just pray Cody was able to save Dawson.

CHAPTER TWENTY-SEVEN

Beckett

The paramedics rush into the room and head straight for Cody, but Corvin won't let her go. Darius hands Leah to Crue and nods to me, the both of us grip Corvin's arms and pull him back so the paramedics can work on Cody. Corv fights us but he can't shake our hold. We watch as they feel for a pulse and begin CPR, the grave looks on their faces tell us what we already know… She's gone.

Time seems to stand still as we stand here and watch the paramedics try everything to bring her back, when the one doing CPR stops and looks at us shaking his head, Corvin collapses in our arms screaming. Darius and I hold Corv through his breakdown and promise him that we will be here by his side and help him through this.

Our house is swarmed by forensic specialists and police, reporters are all stationed outside at the curb of our property like fucking vultures. Cody's body still lays in the game room. We've all been moved into the living room. The cops tried to question us but Saint refused, and said we wouldn't say a word until our lawyer arrived. Troy is on his way now. Saint, Katie and Crue sit on one couch, each of them have their arms around Katie as she cries for her friend. Leah sits on Darius's lap on the other couch with her face buried in his neck crying, I dart my gaze to Corvin who leans against the far wall looking down at the blood that coats his hands.

Fuck, I head into the kitchen to grab the disinfectant wipes Leah stashed in there, the moment I open the door and the light flicks on, a gut-wrenching scream hits my ears and I stumble backward losing my footing and falling to my ass. The moment my eyes land on him, a sob tears out of me.

"Dawson!" I roar, my boy clamps his mouth closed and stares at me for a second before he bursts into tears and runs to me. I wrap him in my arms and hold him tight against me, tears flow down my cheeks knowing that he's okay. I can feel people around us but I don't look up.

"Daddy, I scared, Momma, gone," he cries out. I pull back and meet his stare, his cheeks stained from his tears.

"I know, monster. You were so brave to stay quiet and hide as long as you did," I say.

"Aunt Cody says Dawson has to be shush and no sound. She say not to come out even if she screams. I stay like she said and waited for Daddy, she say Daddy would come save me." I slam my eyes closed and send a silent prayer up to Cody. She fucking gave her life for my son and I will forever be grateful to her because she was a fucking hero.

She saved my boy.

"Aunt Cody is a hero," I whisper as I slowly stand and lift Dawson with me. He clings to me frightened I'll leave him. I look around me to see cops and paramedics standing around, I push past them ignoring their questions as I make my way back into the living room. Everyone looks up at my approach. At the sight of Dawson, they all jump to their feet and each hugs him or tell him how brave he is. I look over to the side to see Corvin standing there still staring at his hands.

"We'll be transporting the body to the morgue for an autopsy." We all turn to see the guy who introduced himself as Detective Anderson standing there. "We will notify the family and will need them to formally I.D the body—"

"Her name is Cody!" Corvin roars from behind us. "Not the fucking body, her fucking name is Cody, use it!" Detective Anderson doesn't seem shocked by Corvin's outburst, he's probably used to it in his line of work. He just nods, apologizes and tells us they will be bringing Cody through in a moment. Dawson reaches for Crue who takes him from me willingly. I keep my eye on him as I move toward Corvin who has gone back to leaning against the wall. I just need all these cops to fuck off so I can get Katie to track Val. Troy walks through the door at that moment. He quickly briefs all of us on what to say, telling us that we'll need to go down to the station and give a statement. I refuse, I'm not going anywhere until I find my girl. All conversation stops as the coroners wheel out a stretcher with a white sheet draped over the top. Katie and Leah both begin to cry at the sight, and Corv rushes forward with me hot on his heels.

"Give them a minute." Detective Anderson says, the two coroners step back, Corv gently pulls the sheet back to reveal Cody's face. A strangled sound escapes him at the sight of her. Corvin's shoulders shake with silent tears, I reach out and place my hand on his shoulder offering him my support.

"I ignored her call. She needed me and I ignored her fucking call." My face slackens, I forgot about him ignoring Cody's calls from earlier today. "I should have been here with her. I broke her fucking heart, Beckett, and now she's gone." He bends down and places a kiss on her forehead. "I should have told you weeks ago that I loved you and now I'll never get the chance to show you just how much you mean to me." He pulls away from her and storms up the stairs without a backward glance. I step forward and look down at my friend.

"Thank you for saving my son, Cody. I'll make sure that

he never forgets the sacrifice you made here today because I know I never will." I bend down and place a kiss on her cold cheek then whisper in her ear. "On my life, I'll make sure whoever the fuck did this dies slowly."

We all pack bags and follow Troy out of the house so the police can close it off as a crime scene, Troy tells us he'll meet us in the morning to go over statements before we head to the station. We all pile into the cars and head to the hotel Troy booked for us, we can't return to the house until the cops finish their investigation. Katie, Saint and Crue ride together in Saint's Jeep, Dawson and I are in my car, while Darius drives Corvin's with Leah.

By the time we pull up to the hotel it's late. Dawson is fast asleep in his seat. I hand my keys to the valet, then grab my son out leaving the others to carry our shit. Saint checks us in and then leads us to the elevators and pushes P. None of us say a word the whole ride up. I'm grateful Corvin showered before we were kicked out of the house. I claim the first bedroom I find and put Dawson to bed, then join the others in the kitchen.

"Katie, I need you to track Val's phone," I say.

"One step ahead of you." I peer around Saint and see Katie sitting at the counter with her laptop in front of her. I know they are all reeling about Cody but I can't focus on that, I need to find Val. "Shit."

I rush forward and peer over her shoulder but none of that shit makes sense to me. "What is it?" I ask.

"Her phone is back at the house. I can't track her, Beck."

"Fuck!" I roar as I scrub a hand down my face, the guys and Leah shoot me pitying looks.

"The cameras, check the cameras from the house," Darius rushes to add. Fuck, how did I not think about that? Just as

Katie gets to work my phone begins to vibrate in my pocket. I pull it out and answer it when I see it's Troy calling.

"What's up?" I say as I bring the phone to my ear.

"Beckett, the PI I put on finding Val's stalker just came back to me." Hope spurs to life inside me.

"What did they find out?" I hear the hope in my own voice, the others stare at me with worried looks.

"We managed to trace back the credit card purchase for the delivery of flowers. It took a shit load of digging but we found him."

"Who the fuck is it?" I growl. Before Troy has a chance to answer Katie speaks.

"Jeff," she breathes his name and points at her screen. Right there in front of me a still frame of Jeff carrying my girl out the front fucking door of my house.

"Beckett, Jeffrey Warner has a long ass list of mental problems. He is unstable so you need to tread carefully," Troy warns.

"Got it," I say as I end the call. "Can you track him?" I ask Katie.

"Already on it, I'll have his location in two minutes," she answers.

"That cunt is going in the ground." Corvin's tone is void of all emotion, his face is etched in pain but it's his eyes, they're filled with bloodlust.

"Guys, you can't just kill someone. Garrett was one thing but there is no way—"

Corvin cuts Leah off. "He killed her!" Corv shouts at her. Leah recoils into Darius who shoots Corvin a glare.

"He doesn't come back alive." All their gazes turn to me but I keep mine on Corvin. "Leah and Katie will stay back and watch Dawson, if the three of you can't stomach what's about to happen, then don't fucking come."

"He took one of ours from us, he doesn't get to breathe when she doesn't. We take the cunt out and make sure Troy has a plan in place to get us off a murder charge," Crue announces, shit, I didn't think about that.

"Leave that with me," Saint says as he walks away with his phone against his ear.

"Darius, please—" Leah pleads but D shakes his head silencing her.

"I love you, Goldie. If the roles were reversed, he would be by my side as I killed the cunt that took you from me. Don't ask me to choose between you and your brother, baby, not tonight, because I don't want to walk out that door while you stand here crying."

I knew without a doubt that my boys would have my back, they are my fucking ride or dies.

CHAPTER TWENTY-EIGHT

Valance

My head feels like a jackhammer is going off inside it, I groan and reach up to rub my temples as I slowly blink my eyes open, only to slam them closed immediately when the light burns my eyes. I try again, blinking them open slowly this time as I sit up. When everything comes into focus I frown, where the hell am I? That's when everything comes back to me and panic sets in. I look around the room, it is bare except for the bed I sit on. I try to block out the pain in my head as I reach down and pat my pockets hoping to find my phone.

"Shit." My pockets are empty. I look to the other side and see a door. I slowly climb to my feet only to fall back down when a wave of dizziness assaults me, I wait until the nauseous feeling passes before I try again. I feel unsteady on my feet and slightly disoriented but the need to get the fuck out of here and get back to Dawson fills me with determination to push through. I fucking pray that Cody was able to get her and Dawson out and get to Beck. My breathing is labored, I try to calm myself down before I grip the door handle and turn.

I'm surprised when the door opens, I expected it to be locked!

I open it just enough to be able to poke my head out and look side to side, there is another that is open opposite me. I slowly creep into the hallway as quietly as I can, melting into the wall on the opposite side and peek into the other room. My eyes widen at the sight of it. There is a race car bed, drawers, and boxes of brand new toys stacked in the corner. This room is for a little boy! A sick feeling begins to settle inside me. I block that out as I slowly creep down the hallway. I stop and take a deep breath as I work up the courage to peer around the corner. The moment I do, my blood runs cold.

I stumble forward, our eyes lock, and he smiles. "Hello, beautiful." I shake my head, this can't be happening, it can't be him! "You must be thirsty, come sit." Unable to move I just stand here. He sighs, then makes his way over to me, gently grips my arm and leads me into the tiny living room that has a small kitchenette off to the side. The thing that does catch my eye as he pushes me into the threadbare sofa is the front door. It can't be more than six feet from me. I look from him to the door wondering if I could outrun him. "It's deadbolted." I snap my gaze back to him only to find him scowling down at me.

"I-I wasn't—"

"Don't lie, Val, it's unbecoming of you." I clamp my mouth closed and watch as he grabs a bottle of water from the fridge, then brings it back to me. I take it, acting on autopilot. I check the seal before unscrewing the top and down half the bottle. "Sorry, Chloroform dehydrates you apparently." The way he says that so casually scares the hell out of me. The fact I can't see Dawson around here eases the fear inside me slightly. He drops into the chair opposite me and smiles. How the fuck he can sit there and act like nothing about this situation is fucking wrong, shows me just how unhinged he is. How did I miss the signs? "Rest up and then we'll go back and get our boy."

My eyes widen. "What?"

His eyes darken. "Dawson needs to be with his mother *and* father." I choke on my own spit. Jeff is out of his fucking mind. He and I have never slept together or even kissed.

"Where is Dawson?" I keep my voice calm and push down my fear. I can't show him how fucking terrified I am. I've seen enough movies to know that the only way I make it out of this unscathed is if I play along and allow him to think I want him as much as he wants me.

"I tried to search for him when I picked you up." He makes it sound like he actually just picked me up instead of knocking me out and drugging me! "But that pesky fucking brunette got in the way." I gasp, he's talking about Cody. "She tried to keep you from me, I had no choice beautiful, you understand that, right?"

I frown, the slight hint of hysteria I detect in his tone has fear clawing its way up inside me. "What do you mean, *you had no choice*?" My tone is even and calm. I act as relaxed as I can, trying to put him at ease enough for him to drop his guard so I can find a way out of here.

"I had to stop her. You belong with me and when she tried to fight me I… I had to stop her but then I panicked and had to leave our boy behind." He's nodding like a maniac, dread pools inside me.

"What did you do to Cody, Jeff?" The tremble in my voice isn't hard to miss, and his eyes implore me to understand. I try to keep my face blank and act noncoherent but it's fucking hard when I am petrified.

"I stabbed her." I cover my mouth with my hand, tears prick the backs of my eyes and I fight to keep them at bay. "I didn't have a choice. I told her if she told me where Dawson was and let me walk out of there with you and him that I wouldn't hurt her. She spat in my face!" he shouts. I recoil into the sofa in fear. "That fucking bitch should have listened!" Tremors overtake my body. I see it now, Jeff is fucking unhinged and there were signs but I ignored them.

He would get angry if I spoke to another guy and he would get upset if I corrected him on Dawson not being his. He would get angry when I told him that I wasn't ready to date or entertain the thought of seeing anyone. Oh my God, I brought this upon myself. I brought this on everyone!

"Why, Jeff, why are you doing all of this?" I hear the defeat in my own voice and I can't bring myself to care. He hurt my friend to get to me, he fucking terrorized me and acted like we were friends. Beck was right, he said Jeff had convenient timing the day the flowers were delivered and I didn't believe him.

"Because I love you, Val. Everything I have done is to show you how much I care… the flowers, the love notes, all of it. I admit, I may have gone a bit overboard with the pictures but I needed you to see that I would do anything for you. Even killing all of those assholes you call friends, especially that juiced up wannabe. I know you must be upset about your friend but we can get you a new one."

I gape at him. "You can't just go and buy people from the store." His face contorts in confusion, holy shit he actually thinks you can just buy people.

"Well, you don't need her, you have me and when we get our son, we'll be a happy family—"

I scoff. "Beckett isn't just going to let *his* son go." He jumps to his feet. I recoil in fear as he reaches into the waist-band of his hands and points a gun at me.

"He isn't his!" he screams. I gulp and honest to God I nearly piss myself. "You and Dawson are mine and if he tries to get in the fucking way of that I'll make sure he'll never bother us again." He closes the space between us and looms above me. I press back into the sofa as far as I can. He reaches out with his free hand to cup my cheek, I flinch away. He growls then grips my hair and yanks it until I'm on my feet in front of him. Tears sting my eyes, I try to stand on my tip toes in the hopes it will ease the pain on my scalp but he yanks me harder, drawing a pained cry from me. "I see now, Beckett has to die."

Call it a blackout or a fit of rage but the moment those words leave his foul mouth it's like a haze overcomes me, then a battle cry that would make any warrior proud leaves me as I attack Jeff. We both fall to the ground. I claw at his face but he bucks his hips and flips us so he's above me. I see him punching me and I sort of feel the ache in my cheek and my side but that's it thanks to the adrenaline coursing through me. My flight or fight instincts kick in the moment he reaches for his gun again. I strike out using the heel of my palm and slam it into his nose. He shouts in pain but it doesn't stop him. I see him lift the gun out of the corner of my eye and the real fight begins.

I grip his arm and try force the gun away from me but he's fucking strong. I buck my hips trying to throw him off balance but he doesn't budge. "If I can't fucking have you, then neither will he!" he yells. I know in this moment that I'm about to lose the fight of my life, he's going to kill me and bury my body somewhere no one will ever find me. Dawson will grow up without a mother and Beck will become a shell of the person he is now because he'll blame himself. He pushes harder and my arms begin to shake as he turns the gun toward me. It's like everything happens in slow motion. I see his finger inching toward the trigger and then the sound of the door being kicked open penetrates the air. Jeff turns and looks over his shoulder.

That moment of distraction costs him, as I turn the gun toward his chest and squeeze the trigger twice. He flicks his gaze back to me in shock as blood begins to seep into his light green shirt.

"Nooo!"

He's here!

Jeff is ripped off me in the next second then Beckett is

there. He reaches for me and I sob the moment he wraps his arms around me. I cling to him and cry, I've never been so fucking scared in my life. I really thought I was going to die tonight and never get the chance to hold my baby again or tell Beck I loved him one last time.

CHAPTER TWENTY-NINE

Beckett

The moment I kicked the door in, took a single step inside the tiny cabin and heard the gunshot, my whole world turned upside down. My heart stopped. Ripping that putrid cunt off her and seeing her still alive and breathing without bullet holes is the only reason my heart started to beat again. She clings to me like she is terrified she'll be taken again. I cup the back of her head and keep her face buried in my chest as I look over to see Corvin on top of Jeff beating the shit out of him, the fact he doesn't even twitch or make a sound tells me he's dead. Good, the cunt doesn't get to live after what he's fucking done. My only hang-up is the fact I wasn't the one to kill him myself.

Crue and Saint drag Corvin off the piece of shit while Darius bends down and holds two fingers against his neck. D cuts a glance to me and shakes his head. A sigh escapes me, how the fuck are we are going to spin this to keep our asses out of jail?

"Someone call 911 now," Saint says. Crue nods at him letting him know he's got Corv and he can let go.

"We can't call the cops," Darius breathes out. Val begins to cry louder and I hold her tighter against me. "We'll go down for this." Val pulls out of my hold and stares up me with panic in her blue eyes.

"I did this. I-I won't let any of you take the blame just look after Dawson—"

"Enough!" Val clamps her mouth closed and buries her face in my chest again at the sound of Saint's raised voice. "No one is going to fucking jail."

"He's dead, dumbass,." I grit out. Saint scowls down at me and shakes his head.

"I know, *dumbass!* Val shot him in self-defense, this isn't a murder charge so call the fucking cops, now!"

Holy shit.

Saint's right, this isn't murder. Val fought for her life and acted in self-defense. Darius makes the call for us. I stand and pull Val to her feet with me, putting some space between us so I can look her over and make sure she isn't injured.

"Are you hurt?" I ask.

She shakes her head and swipes away her tears. "I'm okay, Beck. He has a room back there made up for Dawson." Anger courses through my veins. "He said that he tried to find Dawson but Cody hid him and wouldn't give him up. When she tried to stop him from taking me, he said he stabbed her, is… is she okay?" Her eyes plead for me to tell her that her friend is fine but I can't. A whoosh of air escapes me as I look at Corv, pain is etched across his features at the mention of Cody. Val follows my line of sight and one look at Corvin gives her the answer. "No, no, please God no, not her." I wrap my arms around her and hold her close to me as she breaks down again in my arms. Corv stares at Valance with an angry glint in his eyes and it robs me of air, he blames Val for Cody's death.

It's dawn by the time Detective Anderson lets us go. Darius called Troy and he encouraged us to answer any questions they had, which we did. We need to go down to the station tomorrow and give a formal statement but Anderson says it looks like a cut and dry case to him, which is a fucking relief. We all leave and promise to meet Troy tomorrow at noon to give our statements. Val sits on my lap on the ride home, the ride is quiet and filled with tension. The fact that Saint or Crue haven't cracked a joke tells me that I'm not imagining the tension between Corv and Val.

Darius pulls up out front of the hotel and we all pile out of the car. I wrap my arm around my girl and lead her through the lobby to the elevators. Crue pushes the P as the doors close, and once again the tension amplifies inside the small metal car.

Fuck it.

I dart forward and hit the emergency stop button. The car jolts to a stop and we all stumble a bit. I ignore the other's protests and shouts and I look at Corvin. He stands tall with his fists clenched at his sides. "You get to be pissed, you get to be mad as fuck about what happened to Cody, but you do not get to take it out on her!" I shout as I point toward Val. Corv presses into me and pushes his forehead against mine.

"Don't fucking push me," he snarls.

"It's not her fault," I plead. I see it in his eyes, he needs someone to blame as he sifts his way through the grief and the guilt, and that person is my girl.

"She died because of *her!* She's dead because of *her!*" Val surprises the fuck out of me when she steps out from behind Darius and moves to stand beside me. Corvin refuses to look at her.

"Corvin?" His face twitches in anger but he still won't look at her. "Please, look at me." He growls low in his chest before tearing his gaze from mine to look at Val. I'm poised and ready to fight my best friend if it means stopping him from hurting my girl. "Blame me." I jerk back and look at Val like she's lost her fucking mind. "Latch onto that anger you have toward me, it will help you deal with the pain. It won't fix it or make it easier but trust me when I tell you that blaming me will help you carry on and get out of bed each day. When it comes time for you to finally deal with the pain, come find me because I'll be here waiting." It never dawned on me that Val would be the only person able to relate to what Corvin is going through until this very moment.

"I hate you," Corv snarls.

"I know. You'll hate me for a *long* time but just know you have every right to feel how you do no matter what anyone says. I'm a big girl and I can handle whatever you have to throw at me."

Val steps out of the bathroom in one of my shirts, her hair wet and dripping slightly but she looks more like herself now. The moment we entered the penthouse, Crue and Saint retreated to their room to get some sleep. Corvin stormed off to his room with Darius hot on heels, while I led Val to our room where Dawson was fast asleep on the bed. After kissing him and hugging his sleeping form she wanted a shower. In my haste to get the fuck out of the house, I forgot to pack her some clothes so she's stuck wearing my shit.

"Hey," she says shyly as she makes her way over to the bed where I'm lying with our son.

"Hey," I whisper as she climbs under the covers and smiles at our son, who is fast asleep in the middle of us.

"I thought I would never get to see either of you again." I reach over and cup her cheek, lifting her face until her eyes meet mine.

"We're right here, baby. No one will ever take you from us again." She smiles but it doesn't reach her eyes. It's going to take a long as fuck time for her to feel safe again and that's when it hits me, Corvin needs space and Val needs to get away from here for a while. "What if… what if we went to Alaska for six months like I was meant to?"

Surprise clouds her features. "What?"

"You need to get away for a while and Corvin needs space and honestly, I don't think I would ever feel okay with you or Dawson going back to that house again. You can switch your classes to online so you wouldn't fall behind. I mean, just think of it as a family vacation." Her eyes grow misty with tears.

"Are you sure?" The fact she didn't try to talk me out of it or come up with some bullshit excuse about why we can't go, means she feels the same way I do.

"Yeah, baby. I'll call Shayla in the morning and get her to make the arrangements."

"Who the hell is Shayla?" I fight to keep the smile from my face, even after all the shit she has just been through her only focus is who Shayla is.

"She's the general manager of the resort and oversees the one in Alaska and runs the one in New Zealand and Japan as well." Her eyes narrow. "Babe, she's in her late forties and married to the regional manager of the resort in Alaska as well." Her features smooth out and she smiles sheepishly.

"Well, in that case, that sounds amazing. I think getting away for a while will be good for us, I'm yet to figure out how much the events of today have impacted Dawson." I lean forward and place a kiss on her forehead.

"We'll take it one day at a time."

"Okay. When will we leave?" I mull her question over in my head for a minute.

"We can't leave until Detective Anderson clears us."

"I… I don't want to go until after the funeral, I owe that to… her."

"*We* owe that to her, baby." A tear escapes and slides

down her cheek. "She saved our boy, we'll be there to pay our respects."

"Thank you."

"Try get some sleep. We have a long ass day ahead of us and we need to be up in three hours."

She reaches up and pulls my hand off her cheek and brings it to her lips placing a kiss on each knuckle before meeting my gaze again. "I love you with all my heart, Beckett Dawson."

A grin spreads across my face. "I love you too, Valance Karver." Love shines in her eyes at my words. "I think while we're in Alaska we need to rectify the problem of your name."

"Huh?"

Shooting her a wink as I say. "It's about time you had the same last name as me and our son." Her eyes widen to the size of dinner plates.

"D-did you just ask me to marry you?" she squeaks out, earning a laugh from me.

"Baby I'm not asking you shit, I'm telling you that you *will* be Mrs. Valance Dawson by the end of the year, you best believe that."

EPILOGUE

Beckett

Three weeks later

"Where the fuck is he?" Darius shouts from across the penthouse. I come out of the spare room and growl in frustration.

"He isn't fucking here!" I snap.

Crue and Saint both race down the stairs and shake their heads. "He isn't up there," Saint says.

"Fuck!" I growl out as I scrub a hand down my face. "Darius, you Saint and Crue head to the church."

"Where the fuck are you going?" Crue asks as I grab my suit jacket off the back of the couch where mine, Val and Dawson's bags are all lined up for our flight in the morning. The guys and the girls were shocked by the news when I told them three weeks ago, but they all understood our reasoning and supported our choice, as long as we don't elope and invited them all to the wedding. We got the all-clear from Anderson four days ago and I booked our tickets that night. All we waited on was today, the day we lay Cody Sutton to rest.

"I'm going to pick your girl up so she can track his fucking phone," I answer.

"Wait, I'm coming with you," D calls out as we make our way toward the elevator of the penthouse. We've been given the all-clear to return to our house, but none of us wants to go back there. Corvin can't even spend a day sober so we all know he isn't ready to go back and face that shitshow. He's been spiraling for weeks and won't let any of us help him, he's not going to practice or even keeping up with school. He's just checked out completely.

Darius and I swing by the dorm to pick Katie up, she already has the location up on her phone and rattles off where to go. I white knuckle the steering wheel, frustrated. I knew this would be hard for him but sneaking out the night before the funeral was just reckless. Everyone has been taking Cody's loss fucking hard. Leah and Katie both have been withdrawn and chosen to take their classes online for the remainder of the semester. Katie moved back to the dorm she shared with Cody much to Saint and Crue's dismay. Darius is even considering taking Leah to Chicago for a couple months so he can get a head start in learning the ropes at HQ, he's supposed to head there at the end of the year. He and I both dropped out of the football team last week. Coach was fucking livid but given the news of what happened, he couldn't really argue.

"Remind me again why the hell we are driving around trying to find the man-child?" Katie snarks from the backseat, it's no secret she isn't Corvin's biggest fan after breaking her best friend's heart.

"Because he needs to be there to say goodbye to her," I answer. Katie scoffs.

"Take a right then the first left, it says he's at some motel." I cringe, I don't even want to think about what or who he is doing at the motel. We pull into the carpark and I scrunch my face. It's a fucking dive alright, it looks like one of those motels you pay by the hour for. Katie tells me which room he's in and sure enough, his car is parked out front of room 203. I park the car and step out, Darius following my lead toward the room. I bang on the door loud enough to cause a disturbance.

"Corvin!" I shout as I continue to pound on the door. I'm about to give up and kick it in when it flies open and a tiny, raven-haired girl with bright blue eyes stands before me with a worried look on her face.

"Alexa?" I turn to see Katie behind us with a horrified look on her face as she stares at the girl.

"Fuck," the girl grits out as she shoulders past me and stops a step in front of Katie. "Not a fucking word, I made her a promise and I don't plan on breaking it. He'll fucking pay for what he did." Katie stands there stunned and says nothing as the girl races across the lot and climbs into a beaten-up Honda and speeds away. I duck my head back into the room to see Corvin sitting on the edge of the bed with his face clasped between his hands. I shake off the odd encounter with Katie and the random, just nod to Darius to help me get Corvin's up and in the shower.

We make it to the church with minutes to spare. Corv grumbles as I drag his ass out of the car, luckily Darius thought to bring his suit with us or else he'd be attending this funeral in flip flops and his vomit-covered shirt from last night. Katie shoots Corv a disgusted look before she stomps away from us to take her place inside. I drag Corvin's still, drunk ass into the church. It's packed, the three of us have no choice but to stand in the back. I spot the top of Val's auburn hair up at the front, and my shoulders sag in relief. Each time she is out of my sight I get fucking anxiety and worry myself sick. Our flight tomorrow can't come soon enough.

The priest taps the mic on the podium and draws our attention to the front. I watch Corvin straighten to his full height out of the corner of my eye. His gaze isn't on the priest though, it's on the dark wooden casket that sits up at the front covered in flowers; a large portrait of Cody sits at the head of the coffin on a stand. A lump forms in my throat at the sight of her picture. She was only eighteen, she had her whole life ahead of her and because of some sick fuck her life was robbed from her.

"I can't do this," Corvin mutters, both Darius and I block him from exiting the church.

"You may not want to be here but by God, you are going to stay because that girl deserves that much from you. Man the hell up, Corvin, and pull your head out of your ass. Cody deserves more than this pathetic sack of shit in front of me, don't dishonor her by being a pussy and leaving." I have no words, Darius literally said everything I wanted to say. My attention is pulled to the front when I see a blur of raven-hair. My eyes widen as I watch the raven-haired girl from earlier thank the priest and take his spot on the podium.

"Who the fuck is she?" I growl, low enough for only them to hear.

"Who?" D asks.

"Her!" I grit out as I point at the girl.

"Shit," Darius breathes out at the sight of her, the raven-haired girl lifts her gaze and stares straight at Corvin who stands stiff as a statue beside us. An evil smirk graces the girls face as she stares at Corv, dread begins to form in my stomach. I can feel it, something bad is about to happen.

"Thank you all for coming," she says as she looks around the packed church. "For those of you who don't know me, my name is Alexa." She pulls her stare back to Corvin before she delivers the blow none of us saw coming. "And I'm Cody's little sister."

Oh fuck, Corvin just boned his dead girlfriend's little sister.

Also by Samantha Barrett

PARANORMAL ROMANCE

<u>The Dream Series</u>

<u>The Dream Trilogy</u>

A Beautiful Dream

A Twisted Fate

A Beautiful Nightmare

Redemption

Anarchy

<u>Brutal Savages</u>

Savage Lies

Brutal Truth

Savage Beast

Brutal Beauty

MAFIA ROMANCE

<u>Murdoch Mafia Series</u>

Played By The Bishop

Tormented By The King

Tortured By The Knight

Tempted By The Queen

Turned By The Pawn

Ruined By The Rook

Fairytales With A Twist

Condemned Beast

SPORTS ROMANCE

Playing For Keeps

Duet

Offside

Touchdown

End Game

Hail Mary

Blindside

RH SPORTS

Hate Us Like You Mean It

Acknowledgments

Marcus, I really need to stop saying shit about you in these but until you get off your happy ass and actually read my fucking books, I'll keep putting your ass on blast. Read the fucking book, Marcus, you'd be surprised how much of our sex scenes I use in them!
My Alpha girls, Clare, Sarah and Tash. Thank you ladies from the bottom of my cold fucking dead heart, these books wouldn't be what they are without all your help and feedback, thank you and I love you!
My Army, Alicia, Amber, Angel, Ash, Barb, Charlotte, Cyndi, Debbie, Jasmine, Jen, Kahanna, Katelyn, Lakshmi, Lora, Lyndsey, Sarmi and Tess. Thank you ladies so fucking much for being the best freaking team an author could ask for, I owe you all so much for the love and dedication you give me.
My ASSistant, Tash (did you see what I did there lol). All jokes aside, thank you babe for all that you do for me, your work doesn't go unnoticed that is for sure, love ya.
My editor, Lizz, fucking hell you are amazing! Thank you so much for continuing to love each of my books and making them all pretty for me. You truly are a star my friend.
My sprint partner, Jaye Pratt. Thank you for writing with me each day and listening to meltdowns when I cried over Cody dying and helping me plot.
My demon spawn, my children, my heartbeats. I love you with everything that I am and cherish both of you more than you will ever know.
Leah Maree, my love, as per usual you smashed this fucking

cover out of the park. You are so beyond talented and I am in
awe of you.
My parents, dear lord, I hope you never read these books,
Dad, because I would never be able to look you in eye again!
Mum, thank you for always supporting and loving me.
Last but not least, you, my amazing readers mean everything
to me! Without you none of this would be possible, thank you
for your continued support and reading my books, it still
stuns me to get messages from you telling me you love my
books. I really am living my dream and that's thanks to you.
Sam

About the Author

Samantha Barrett is a dark romance, PNR author who loves to write out-of-the-box stories. She is originally from the land of the long white cloud, New Zealand. She is totally fluking her way through this whole author gig, if she isn't writing you can find her kicking back with her kids and husband with a bag of chips and a glass of wine in her hand.
Sam loves Twilight and is a TWIHARD proudly.